D0416099

ASK FOR THE MOON

ASK FOR THE MOON

SHIRLEY GEE

faber and faber

LONDON · BOSTON

First published in 1987 by
Faber and Faber Limited
3 Queen Square London WC1N 3AU

Photoset by Wilmaset Birkenhead Wirral
Printed in Great Britain by
Redwood Burn Ltd Trowbridge Wiltshire
All rights reserved

© Shirley Gee 1987

All rights whatsoever in this play are strictly reserved
and professional applications for permission to perform it, etc.
must be made in advance, before rehearsals begin, to
David Higham Associates Ltd,
5–8 Lower John Street, Golden Square,
London W1R 4HA.

Amateur applications for permission to perform
must be made in advance, before rehearsals begin, to
Samuel French Ltd, 52 Fitzroy Street,
London W1P 6JR.

*This book is sold subject to the condition that it shall not,
by way of trade or otherwise, be lent, resold, hired out
or otherwise circulated without the publisher's prior consent
in any form of binding or cover other than that in which
it is published and without a similar condition including this
condition being imposed on the subsequent purchaser.*

British Library Cataloguing in Publication Data

Gee, Shirley
Ask for the moon.
I. Title
822'.914   PR6057.E2/

ISBN 0–571–13875–6

For Joby,
our son and a lovely lad

There is no present or future – only the past, beginning over and over again – now.

Eugene O'Neill, *A Moon For The Misbegotten*

I walked through the market and I saw our dress. £1.50 I got for it. They're selling them for £16.99.

Overlocker, 1986

It makes me miserable to be so badly paid. I feel I'm no use in the world or else they'd pay me more.

Seamstress, 1890

The dress of a young bride is made of soft textured silk or satin or brocade, trimmed with flowers and rich white lace and a large, ornate veil of the same description of lace as on the dress.

Sunday at Home, 1872

Every day putting the cloth through the machine. I feel it. The tiredness. The long hours of noise. The tiredness builds, the noise builds, the radio, the machine. Ten tablets a day I take. Blood pressure. Explain me, please, I said, what is this pressure in the blood. You wouldn't understand if I told you, he said.

Machinist, 1986

> Needlepin, needlepin, stitch upon stitch,
> Work the old lady out of the ditch.
> Hang her up for half an hour,
> Cut her down just like a flower.
> I won't be hung for half an hour,
> I won't be cut down like a flower.
>
> A lace tell

O God, what am I going to say to him? I really shake inside. I do everything, housework, work, everything. I don't know why I don't collapse and give up. I don't know how I got that strong will-power to survive. Maybe I got my children, that give me the reason. I have to feed them. I have to give them proper home. I must make them strong. It's been a bad day and he's coming and I'm not ready. O dear God.

Homeworker, 1986

To Love And Live Happy That Is My Desire.
I Wants A Husband.
My Love As Broken My Poor Hart.
Jesus Wept.
When This You See Remember Me And Bear Me In Your Mind.

Lace bobbin inscriptions

'I hit the child with a mallet. It were no good for it to live too long. I made a proper muddle of it, though. I should do it better next time. I wrapped it in William's second best shirt, sir.'
'William?'
'My brother, sir. It weren't his best shirt of course, sir. I wouldn't have used his best, sir.
'Yes, yes. Continue.'

Court report, 1836

Pieceworkers are now guaranteed at least the same rate as timeworkers no matter what their speed is, provided they are members of a union. However, the law does not protect the ignorant.

National Union of Tailors and
Garment Workers spokesman, 1987

When you have no organization, no parity of bargaining, the good employer is undercut by the bad and the bad by the worst – where these conditions prevail you have not a condition of progress but a condition of progressive degeneration. The degeneration will continue, and there is no reason why it should not continue in a sort of squalid welter for a period which compared with our brief lives is indefinite.

Winston Churchill, 1909

CHARACTERS

The Laceworkers
FANNY   sixteen, from Devon
MERCY   twenty, from the same village as Fanny
ALICE   twenties, from Nottingham

The Sweatshop
LIL   elderly, white
CARLIE   mid-forties, black
ANWHELA   late twenties, Asian
EUGENE   forties, white

The Laceworkers' time scale runs from dawn, February 1840, to dusk, February 1842. The Sweatshop time scale runs from 8 a.m. to 8 p.m. on a Monday in February at the present time.

Unless an exit is specified, the LACEWORKERS remain on stage throughout.

Ask for the Moon was first performed at the Hampstead Theatre, in September 1986. The cast was as follows:

The Laceworkers
FANNY   Jane Horrocks
MERCY   Victoria Burton
ALICE   Gaylie Runciman

The Sweatshop
LIL   Brenda Bruce
CARLIE   Mona Hammond
ANWHELA   Shireen Shah
EUGENE   Brian Hall

Director   John Dove
Designer   John McMurray
Lighting   Brian Harris

The sweatshop is crammed with boxes, crates, rolls of material, cardboard patterns hung in rows, an ironing board, the floor a jumble of scraps and cut-offs. Three industrial sewing machines. Cobwebs. Dust. A cramped and crumbling room. If there is a window, most of it is blocked with cardboard. Piles of skirts, cheap trousers, overalls, cheap fabrics. A sense of other rooms above, next door, below. The phone rings frequently in another room. Sometimes there is Radio 1.

The lacemakers' cottage – a small stone room. At night candle-lit, lamp-lit. Stools and lace pillows for the three to work at. A sense that outside there is space and air. Inside not so much. The women work in a half-circle. There is a firepot on the floor.

Sometimes the action might take the SWEATSHOP WORKERS into the Victorians' territory, sometimes the LACEWORKERS may flow into the sweatshop.

LIL should always wear her overcoat until she strips. She is not self-pitying, ever; she kicks. She and CARLIE fight their war against the bitter cold, against pain in back, eyes, fingers, against the clock, with panache, gallantry and light-heartedness wherever possible. ANWHELA has a quieter courage. EUGENE, also a fighter, as much a victim as the others, is either on tenterhooks or slumped.

MERCY coughs with increasing pain as the play progresses. She is still the strongest, in charge. Her illness gives her a restless vitality. FANNY, impatient, ready for laughter, is still free, alert, hungry for life. ALICE is an outsider despite having lived some years in the village. Her body a stiff question-mark, she has to bend closer and closer to her work to see it. Again, there is no trace of self-pity in any of them. They are all proud of what they do. They know there is a price to pay.

Everyone in the play shares the fear of time – the ceaseless consciousness of minutes saved, minutes lost.

ACT ONE

The laceworkers' cottage. Early February, 1840. A cold dawn.
MERCY *is sitting at her stool, already working at the lace.* FANNY
and ALICE *enter shivering, yawning.*

FANNY: Look at that sky.

ALICE: My feet is stones.

FANNY: The moon's still up.

ALICE: Where's the life gone in this fire?

FANNY: Reckon I've a year's sleep left in me.

ALICE: Wish it was Sunday.

FANNY: You say that every bloody morning, Alice. Every –

MERCY: Come on, come on.

> (ALICE *and* FANNY *go to their stools, sit, blow on their hands,
> bend over their work. Freeze.*)

The sweatshop. Early February: 8 a.m., now. CARLIE *and* LIL *are
on their machines. The third chair at the third table is empty. They
shout above the roar.*

LIL: How long till tea, Carlie?

CARLIE: About a month.

LIL: Them last lot was a doddle, wasn't they? Raced through
them like a mouse through a minefield. Wonder if it's
sunny? Said on the telly it would be. But that weatherman,
he gets so panicky.

CARLIE: We'll never know.

LIL: What you dreaming about, Carlie? Your next man?

CARLIE: My Saturday shopping.

LIL: It's a million miles to Saturday.

> (*The machines roar. Stop. The lights cross-fade.*)

The laceworkers' cottage. The LACEWORKERS *working on their stools.*

FANNY: It's a year to bedtime. Stumpy had a bullcalf in the
night. Didn't get no sleep at all.

MERCY: Least you're snug in that hayrack. Get warmth from
the beasts.

ALICE: I'm cosy enough now, nights. Started sleeping with my
sister and her husband. Saves on the bedding, too.

MERCY: What happen when they —
ALICE: I roll over.
FANNY: Wishes it were her.
　　(*They laugh.*)
MERCY: Now Fanny, get on. Alice.
FANNY: How long we got?
　　(*Swift cross-fade.*)

The sweatshop. The machines start up again. They shout.
LIL: How long we got?
CARLIE: Long enough.
LIL: I'm dying to blow my nose.
CARLIE: Well, blow it then.
　　(*They adjust material.*)
LIL: It's not included on my agenda, love.
CARLIE: Just don't blow it on a sleeve.
LIL: I'll blow it on your drawers if you don't watch it.
　　(*They machine.*)
　　I'll have to stop, it's no use. (*Does, blows her nose.*) Oh,
　　lovely. I'd rather see a church fall down than wait that long
　　again.
　　(CARLIE *stops a moment, stands, rubs her back.*)
CARLIE: Those two old prunes upstairs are still away.
LIL: Why do you always have a go at them?
CARLIE: Can't stand them. They're never here – their backs or
　　their eyes or their feet or they've broken their glasses. Time
　　they tottered off.
LIL: (*As they both turn on their machines, yelling happily above the
　　roar*) I'm not stopping till I'm stopped.

*The laceworkers' cottage. Late morning, late February, 1840. A
hammering at the door. A tension runs through the* VICTORIANS.
They draw in their breath a moment, gather themselves. MERCY
rises.
MERCY: Fogerty!
　　(*She hurries out.* ALICE *scuttles into the shadows, but* FANNY
　　catches her by the arm.)
FANNY: After you, is he?

(ALICE *shrinks*.)
Found you out? (*Laughing, she lets* ALICE *go*.) No, it's the
veil. I got this funny feeling in the night. Old bastard
Fogerty's going to do it, going to choose –
ALICE: Sh– !
(*They both listen*.)
He's going.
(MERCY *comes back in*.)
FANNY: Well?
MERCY: Well . . . it's us, then.
(FANNY *gives a cry of delight, swings* MERCY *round*.)
FANNY: I knew it. Didn't I say I had a feeling –
MERCY: (*Hugging* FANNY *back*) He say it must be perfect.
FANNY: It will be.
(ALICE *moves in towards them, the three of them filled with
suppressed excitement*.)
MERCY: He say Squire's daughter say it must be exquisite. I say
to Fogerty, tell her not to fret herself. We know what we're
about.
FANNY: She'll be beautiful all right if we're the ones to put it all
together.
ALICE: Dorcas tell me Squire's daughter's got three travelling
trunks full of all her trousseau. Dorcas has seen inside one.
MERCY: ⎫ No!
FANNY: ⎭ What?
ALICE: Six shifts, she says, summer vests and winter, woollen
stockings, silk stockings, lisle stockings, lace stockings. Six
pair of boots, just for bad weather. Six dozen
handkerchiefs, Mercy, three dozen for common use, three
dozen for finer, and lace ones besides –
FANNY: She'll be all right then if she cry.
MERCY: Come on, Alice.
FANNY: Alice'll keep up.
(*They sit to work*.)
We'll make a veil so light a breath'll raise it and sigh'll let it
fall.
MERCY: Mind your stitch, Fan.
(*A silence*.)

3

ALICE: Oh, my feet. My chilblains is driving me to screaming.

MERCY: Never mind your feet, use your hands.

ALICE: Haven't had a laugh all week.

(*A whistle outside the door.* FANNY *is instantly alert.*)

MERCY: I see you, Fanny.

FANNY: That's Jacob –

MERCY: Sit.

(*Another whistle.*)

FANNY: (*Starting to rise*) It might be a signal –

MERCY: Sit!

(FANNY *sits.*)

We've to have the best part of this done by the end of June. That give us only five month. Near enough. So get your head down. I'll give you a laugh, Alice. Fanny's running after Jacob fast as she can go.

FANNY: You've a nose as long as a carrot, Mercy. Always poked in my affairs.

ALICE: Fixed on him, have you?

FANNY: Lord – !

MERCY: I know Fan. She gaze deep into a boy's eyes. Like she could see the bottom of his soul. And all she's thinking of is her next meal. Will it be bread and scrape or will she get a bit of bacon.

FANNY: (*Taunting them*) A bacon and potato pie. Can't hardly get your mouth round it.

ALICE: Lord, Fanny, you'll make me faint with wanting.

FANNY: A big slab of it. And onion. Bacon, tate and onion –

MERCY: Fanny, mind your work –

FANNY: Juice all dripping down your fingers, down your chin –

MERCY: (*With urgency now*) Mind, I said. You lose your stitch, we're done.

The sweatshop. A long run on the machines. They stop. Adjust.

LIL: Saw that bloke again last night. Ever seen him?

CARLIE: What you on about now?

LIL: That bloke. On *Top of the Pops*. You know.

(*They machine, stop, adjust.*)

CARLIE: What's his name?

LIL: Don't know.

CARLIE: What's he look like?

LIL: He jumps about. Gets on your nerves.

(*They machine, stop, adjust.*)

CARLIE: Talking of nerve, you're buggering that up.

LIL: I'm not.

CARLIE: Any bet you like.

LIL: Done.

CARLIE: Ten p.

LIL: Forty thousand quid.

CARLIE: Done.

LIL: Of the tax-payers' money.

CARLIE: Go on, then.

(LIL *holds up her work. She has sewn two trouser legs together end to end.*)

LIL: Oh Gawd.

CARLIE: Shit, Lil.

LIL: Well, two for the price of one.

CARLIE: Bloody hell, Lil.

LIL: I know. I'm all over the place today. (*Starting to unpick her mistake*) It's Maurice, Carlie. He's ill.

CARLIE: Again?

LIL: Friday night it started. He just lay down by his litter tray –

CARLIE: Don't you start laying down on me. Naseem's trouble enough. Better move her stuff –

(EUGENE *races in, trips over a large battered suitcase.* LIL *slips her mistake away from* EUGENE'S *sight and puts a fresh garment in her machine.*)

EUGENE: What's this?

LIL: Eugene, can I use the phone?

EUGENE: What is it?

CARLIE: It's Naseem's.

LIL: Can I?

EUGENE: Use the phone? That phone's our lifeline. It's the arterial nerve centre of this whole enterprise. What's it doing here?

LIL: She thinks they're on to her. The Council.

EUGENE: (*Kicking the case*) It's no good to me here.

LIL: She's got all her stuff in there.

EUGENE: Fire hazard.

CARLIE: Don't make me laugh.

EUGENE: It's blocking up the passageway, Carlie. It's dangerous.

LIL: Got her whole life in there. That's what she said. It's Maurice. He's ill. He's with the Blue Cross now. They said to phone –

EUGENE: When you've done that lot. And not until. God knows you're behind. We're all behind. Four times I've had Mr Sharma on to me about this lot. Yelling threats. He's sixteen stone, that man. Pulse like a child of ten. One tap I'd be in traction. I shouldn't have to use the phone like that, not with my throat. (*Yelling*) NASEEM!

CARLIE: She's on the toilet, Eugene.

EUGENE: Course she's on the toilet. Everyone in this place is always on the toilet. (*Tries to lift the case.*) She got her kids in here or what?

LIL: Show me a body in a trunk and I'll show you a sloppy packer.

EUGENE: I'm not having her lumbering this place up with her wreckage. NASEEM!

CARLIE: She's due to be slung out of her home.

EUGENE: I'm sorry, but she shouldn't have got herself into this situation. Squatting. At her age.

CARLIE: She got behind.

LIL: Once you're behind, even five or six quid behind, you're on the run for life.

EUGENE: NASEEM! (*As he dashes off, lugging the case*) She's probably moving her kids into my toilet right now.

CARLIE: I love all that about a fire hazard. That case is full of soup tins. Be the only thing in this whole place that wouldn't end a stick of charcoal.

LIL: Blocking up the passageway, he said. It's a long time since anyone's blocked my passageway.

CARLIE: Bloody hell.

LIL: You nearly smiled. How long to tea break? Poor old Naseem.

6

(LIL's *machine jams*.)
Oh, bugger. (*Tries to mend it.*) Maurice and me'll be
squatting soon. Had the fire engines round again last week.
CARLIE: I know. You told me. Some rotten bugger's pinched
my chalk.
(*The phone goes in Eugene's office.*)
LIL: I got to get on that phone.
CARLIE: (*Shouting*) Vi! You swiped my chalk? (*To* LIL) I'll get
it. (*As she leaves*) By the time she's crept her way over I'll
have reincarnated.
(LIL *sits a moment, absent-mindedly wiping her eyes on a spare
trouser leg, overwhelmed with worry over her cat, the extra
work if Naseem should go, falling behind, her mistakes.
Suddenly she rises, takes some garments from her pile of finished
work, including her mistake, and quickly crosses to* CARLIE's
place. She exchanges these garments for some from CARLIE's
finished work. Straightens everything hurriedly as she hears
CARLIE *returning.*)
LIL: (*To herself*) Sorry, Carlie.
CARLIE: (*Off*) Shake out your piggy bank, Vi. Buy your own.
(CARLIE *sits down at her place. She chalks some garments.*)
LIL: I've got a lovely cheese roll for dinner. It's that nice soft
bread, not one of them bloody granite things. She picked it
out for me. You can have a bit.
(CARLIE *turns to check her pile of finished work for a moment.*
LIL *rushes to distract her. She succeeds.*)
My dad, Carlie, he had this bit of chalk. Used to chalk it on
the fireplace for my mum. 'Get The Coal In.' 'Clean My
Boots.' He was the bastard of the world. Wouldn't give you
a word, let alone a sixpence. Mean as a guard dog.
CARLIE: There's marriage for you.
LIL: Thought you was all for it. All them kids.
CARLIE: I buried my marriages a long time ago, love. A long
time ago.
LIL: Bet you miss it, though.
CARLIE: Sooner wear a vest.
LIL: What, you?
Ooo ahh

I've lost my bra
I wonder where
My knickers are.
That's you.

CARLIE: Bollocks.

LIL: Ooh ahh.

CARLIE: Double bollocks. Lyle's dad was on to me the other night. Start afresh, he says. No chance, I says. You'll never even get the top button undone. So first it's floods of tears, two minutes later he's got the kids and me bouncing off the walls, looping the loop. Got my own back, though. Hid his teeth. Had him on his knees to me.

LIL: I love your life.

CARLIE: Try living it.

LIL: Wish I could.

CARLIE: Just dying for it, aren't you?

LIL: Well, why not?

CARLIE: It isn't nice at your age, that's why not. It's rude.

LIL: You want us creeping about in lavender, is that it? Not supposed to hear the music when you're old, are you? Not even tap your foot. Dump all your feelings in the deep freeze. Oh, never mind. We'll all be cut down like the grass one of these days. Even you.

(LIL *wipes her eyes on a garment.*)

CARLIE: Don't *do* that.

LIL: Oh, there I go again.

CARLIE: Bloody stupid.

LIL: Just it was to hand.

CARLIE: Well, don't.

LIL: My eyes are watering all the time. Where are my scissors? Running damp, eh? I'm like this place. Falling apart. (*Searching on her table*) Hiding on me, are you, scissors? Bastard things have walked again. (*As she wanders off*) I had them when I . . . didn't I . . . or did I . . .

(CARLIE *turns her attention back to her pile of finished work, freezes as the lights come up on the* VICTORIANS.)

The laceworkers' cottage. June 1840.

MERCY: Right, then.

(*She unwraps lace bundles that other* LACEWORKERS *in the village have brought to her cottage to be incorporated into the veil.*)

FANNY: Let's see.

(*They gather round, pore over the pieces, examine them expertly.*)

MERCY: Mrs Inshaw's, that scroll work.

ALICE: She's a queen at it. Tell her stitch anywhere.

FANNY: Hear the men singing in the high field? Old Tom?

(*They listen a moment.*)

Look at that. That's the *bullock's heart*. First time I seen that. That Greenwood's there, or Sophie Judkins' lot?

MERCY: Greenwood's.

FANNY: It's good. It's going to be good, Merce. Leaving out this, of course. Any money in the world this is Kate Cobb's. Can't stand her stitching. Limp and horrible.

ALICE: You seen her dance? She can dance like an angel.

FANNY: Oh, she's all right when she dance. It's when she stitch. Look at her leaf there, all jagged. Give me a pain in the belly. There's Jacob.

(*A voice rises above the others. They listen.*)

Don't he sing true?

MERCY: He've got a voice like a corncrake.

FANNY: Sun's shining out there. Bet his arms is brown as loaves.

MERCY: Stop dwelling on him. You hadn't gone mooning after him last week we'd all be out there now.

ALICE: Jacob and you —

FANNY: Shut your mouth, bloody Alice.

MERCY: Couple of minutes under a hedge, you got us all in trouble.

FANNY: Four minutes late, that's all. Four little minutes. Fogerty's mean as winter.

MERCY: That he may be, but what he say go. Come on.

FANNY: Well, I'm going in the long grass dinnertime and no one's going to stop me.

MERCY: Now, Fan, you know what he say.

FANNY: Take my boots off. Have a run. You should come.

9

MERCY: No, Fanny. No risks. Not now. No risks.
(*The* LACEWORKERS *bend over their work.*)

The sweatshop. 10 a.m. EUGENE *roars in.* CARLIE *turns to him.*
EUGENE: Rene says we won't get a full docket out of the brown.
CARLIE: Why?
EUGENE: It's damaged. Damaged. God, I feel damaged all over.
Oh my God, why is it always me? I try to do some good in
this world. I'm fully paid up with my VAT almost. I'm
keeping all my dear old ducks afloat – Where's Lil?
CARLIE: Lost her scissors.
EUGENE: Again? I'm going to have to let her go, Carlie. If she
can't keep up. I don't know how the hell I'm going to do it,
she's been here since before the railways came, but –
CARLIE: What are you going to do about the brown?
EUGENE: Don't keep asking me, twisting the knife. I don't
know, do I?
(LIL *is heard off, laughing.*)
LIL: (*Off*) Do you mind?
EUGENE: (*As* LIL *re-enters, muttered to* CARLIE) Keep an eye on
her. (*To* LIL) Rene says we won't get a full docket out of
the brown, Lil.
LIL: Oh God. Why?
EUGENE: It's damaged.
LIL: Oh look. Here they (*the scissors*) were all the time. Led me a
right dance, you little buggers. Why don't you lop an inch
off the bottom?
EUGENE: What?
LIL: Lop some. Off the bottom.
CARLIE: Brilliant.
LIL: You'll have to, won't you?
EUGENE: (*Dizzy with happiness*) Lil, you little raver.
(*He picks her up and swings her round.*)
Think we'll get away with it?
LIL: Wouldn't be the first time. Remember the tartan A-lines?
We had this cutter, Carlie, with a wonky leg, always
sucking spangles –
EUGENE: Walking encyclopedia, this one.

LIL: Irreplaceable, aren't I.

EUGENE: Darling, you're here because you've got such a lovely bum. (*Pats it.*)

LIL: Cheeky. Still your best girl, am I?

EUGENE: That's it. Hey, watch what you're doing, Rene said last week you chopped a –

LIL: Bloody Rene. Lop an inch off her bottom. I got the answer there, though, haven't I?

CARLIE: Has Rene tested it for shrinkage?

EUGENE: That's a point.

LIL: Better pray minis make a come-back.

EUGENE: I'll go and check with her.

(*He rushes off.* CARLIE *starts to count her unfinished pile of work.*)

LIL: His dad had that exact same look. Under the eyes. When there was a bit of muddle on. Used to have his table right where you are now. Humming away, doing the lay-out. 'Roses of Picardy'. Always the same. Drove us all bananas.

CARLIE: Must have.

LIL: Oh, we loved him though. 'How's my best girl?' – that's what his dad called me –

CARLIE: (*Counting the garments*) That's funny . . .

LIL: 'His best girl'.

CARLIE: I could have sworn . . .

(LIL *notices and is alarmed. She hovers round* CARLIE, *pulls her sleeve.*)

LIL: Tea break minus four . . . three . . . two . . . one . . . ZERO.

(*The bell rings.*)

I'll make it.

CARLIE: That's really weird.

LIL: Tea break, Carlie. Didn't you hear? I volunteered you a cup of tea. Carlie?

(*She tugs at* CARLIE.)

CARLIE: Fuck. I keep losing count.

(LIL *races to a bale of material, drapes it round her, poses.*)

LIL: How do I look, eh?

(LIL *clowns around.*)

CARLIE: Diabolical.

(LIL *puts a pair of trousers on her head.*)

LIL: Better? Carlie? Is it? Oh, come on –

CARLIE: (*Successfully distracted*) If it's style you're after –
(*She wraps a bolt of cloth round her Afro-style. Parades. Enjoys herself.*)

LIL: Here, show me, Carlie. Let me try.

CARLIE: You got to swan around. Own the world. Follow me.
(LIL, *relieved, tries to copy* CARLIE. *Then starts to enjoy it too. They waltz, they preen. Finally* CARLIE, *with* LIL *dotting about behind her, swoops off trailing a long, dusty swathe of cheap material which drags across the stage.* LIL *at the last moment turns, sees Carlie's pile. Frozen with guilt and misery she stares at it.*)

The laceworkers' cottage. As the sweatshop material swishes off in the wake of CARLIE, *the* VICTORIANS *with tender care unfold their completed bride's veil.*

FANNY: Oh Lord.

MERCY: Don't it shine, though.

FANNY: It's a living thing.

ALICE: Fanny, that's the truth.
(*The veil is now stretched out between them. In silence they gaze at it, turn it to the light, touch it gently.*)

FANNY: Oh Lord, oh Lord.

MERCY: I'll not forget this. Never.

ALICE: I was married once. Before I come here.

MERCY: Well, you're a dark horse.

FANNY: You've never spoke of it.

ALICE: Nothing to tell. He was a wool carder.

MERCY: God, the last thing in this world I'd ever be.

ALICE: A wall fell on him. Crushed him. Never had a new dress since that dress when I was married. Squire's lady gave me a black dress belonged to some old aunt but I don't like to wear it. It's rusted. Clammy under the arms.

FANNY: See the *great running river* there, winding all around?

ALICE: Yeh. Beautiful.

MERCY: And the little waves, the little bumps the light and shadow fall on.

FANNY: Yeh.

ALICE: Makes you want to cry. (*Running her hand gently along part of the veil, seeing the calendar of their months of work in it*) Started in February, March I was sick, caught up in April, June was the *sprigs*, August Kate Cobb died, edges, September, October, November – that's quick.

FANNY: (*Dreaming*) Come spring Jacob'll take me by the hand – (MERCY *and* ALICE *tense suddenly. The veil, which had hung quite loose between* FANNY *holding it at one end and* MERCY *at the other, stretches between them, taut.*)

MERCY: Do he know?

FANNY: Not yet.

MERCY: Love and work don't mix.

FANNY: I'll get him round to it, you'll see.

ALICE: No sign yet. He hardly looks at you.

FANNY: He have his eye on the horizon.

MERCY: Do he have his feet on the ground?

ALICE: Made a woman of you yet, Fan?
(FANNY *stares at* MERCY, *challenging her. A silence. Then –*)

MERCY: What are we doing here? The minute that clock strike Fogerty'll crack his stick down on that door – come on.
(*They fold the veil, differences forgotten, as fast as possible.*)

ALICE: He'd do you better, Fan. Old Fogerty. He's hot for you. They say he's a bag of sovereigns under his apple tree.

FANNY: He's a wicked bastard and one day I'll tell him so.

MERCY: He's all right.

FANNY: He's what?

MERCY: Where'd we be without him, that's the thing. When my family was all took off with fever he could have threw me out, but no.

FANNY: Only because he knew you work like a dog.
(MERCY *holds the folded veil.*)

MERCY: Do I want to be without my cottage? You want to find yourself without a place to work? Do you? You stitch your lips together, Fan. All right sleeping rough in barns and hayracks, your strength haven't all gone in the lace, but you couldn't work there, could you? Alice's kin haven't an inch to spare between them. So you stitch your lips. We'll just do what he say and what he want. Have it ready, have it right. Now wrap it.

(*A short silence. They bundle it in two layers of cloth, a layer of sacking.*)

ALICE: Fogerty wears gloves in bed.

FANNY: What?

ALICE: He does. Dorcas Parkin ran to fetch a doctor to him once when he was sick. She seen him up against his pillows, picking at the sheets. He'd gloves on.

FANNY: Imagine his old hands in his old gloves. Touching you.

ALICE: All over you.

MERCY: (*Drawn in, despite herself*) His turkey neck.

ALICE: Eyes all water.

MERCY: His old thing like a limp wet rag.

FANNY: Have to take a telescope to see it. I'd sooner do a week's bundle of lace. I would.

ALICE: I would too.

FANNY: Sooner marry the pigman.

ALICE: Think what's under his tree.

FANNY: Wouldn't give you a farthing for him, or his gold. Give a lot to see her, though. The bride. See her pass by.

ALICE: I would too.

MERCY: Satin and flowers and rich white lace.

(*They have completely lost their sense of urgency.*)

FANNY: Put it on me.

MERCY and ALICE: (*Together*) What?

FANNY: I'll wear it. So we can see. Go on.

ALICE: Mercy? Should we?

MERCY: Shall we, though?

FANNY: Oh, come on.

(*Careful, fearful, with delight, they unfold the veil again and drape it over FANNY. Arrange it. Drink it in.*)

MERCY: We done it right.

ALICE: It's like a mist.

FANNY: A breath'd raise it –

MERCY: And a sigh'd let it fall.

FANNY: Look at me. I'm shaking.

ALICE: So am I.

MERCY: That's worked out, that *honeysuckle twine* along the
fall.
(FANNY *slowly sways, moves, walks in it. The bride. Holding
her train,* ALICE *and* MERCY *move too. They are all caught in a
dream.*)
ALICE: Never seen so much lace to a body.
MERCY: Keep us all three fed and clothed for life. God. That's
the church clock struck.
(*They take the veil off in panic, rush to fold it, giggling, though
still with care.*)
Quick. Oh quick.
(MERCY *exits with the veil. Fogerty's stick thunders on the door.*)

The sweatshop. After the tea break. CARLIE *enters, puts the bale back
in place.*
EUGENE: (*Off*) Lil!
(*He roars in.*)
LIL: Here comes the galloping thimble. How's your throat?
EUGENE: Terrible. Like a pin cushion.
LIL: Things always go straight to his throat. Remember when
you had the croup? – I'm sat on the floor, Carlie, him in my
arms, under the cutting table like a little house – remember?
EUGENE: Yeah, I do. Girls, do these yokes. Don't bother to press
them.
(LIL *and* CARLIE *stare at him, appalled.*)
CARLIE: What's the matter with these, then?
EUGENE: Some bloody outworker's done them all wrong.
CARLIE: It's their fault. Let them do it.
EUGENE: There's a whole batch. It'll take too long.
CARLIE: Sod it, Eugene –
EUGENE: I haven't time to argue. I've Blockman's on the line,
they're foaming blood.
(*He gives* CARLIE *a quick, hopeful kiss and races off* –)
Go on, I'll make it up to you. Naseem's gone. I'm short.
CARLIE: It's us that's short.
(*Furious, she slams the extra work into two piles, one for her, one
for* LIL, *chalking them as she does so.*)
LIL: Hey, that's Naseem bit the dust. Those toads up the Council

won't help her either. They don't care. Our place is terrible. Told you about my pilot light, didn't I? No wonder it goes out, I said, the corridor's so bloody draughty the carpet's flapping up and down like the sea. One day Maurice and me'll wake up and find ourselves gassed to death. They don't care. They think you're being awkward. They're all toads.

CARLIE: You got those (LIL's *own workpile*) ready yet?

LIL: In my own sweet time.

CARLIE: This cloth's so bloody rotten you can put your hand through it. It's a pig to work under pressure.

LIL: We used to make some lovely things. Quality things. In Eugene's father's time. Ruching. Cross-stitch. Smocking. Told you about my smocking, didn't I – that prize I won? You could tell our things, even on the hanger. It's the line. The secret's in the line.

CARLIE: He's a lousy pattern-cutter, Eugene. Come on, Lil, for God's sake. We got all Naseem's lot to get through.

LIL: This place was crammed with girls, we had next door as well. You should have seen us, Carlie, rows of us, heads bent, hands flying.

CARLIE: You're going to hold me up.

LIL: Don't panic.

CARLIE: I'm not panicking. I'm waiting. I'm WAITING.

LIL: (*Still not sitting, still not starting work, deliberately challenging* CARLIE) The day I got my first rise I put a penny – that's an old penny – up on the wall between the railings. That'll still be there. The girls have gone but that'll be there all right. Girls have come and girls have gone but *I* stay on for ever.

(*And slowly, deliberately, she sits and starts to machine.*)

CARLIE: For Christ's sake, Lil –

LIL: I'm rattling along. Got the two-minute mile here. There we are. (*Holds up a garment.*) Is this right? It don't look right somehow.

(*She holds it up. The fringing hangs in loops. It's terrible.*)

CARLIE: I don't believe it.

LIL: I hate the stuff. Thought it looked wonky. I said, didn't I?

CARLIE: I bloody don't believe it.

LIL: (*Wrapping it round her head*) As worn by Princess Anne?

CARLIE: Eugene'll go spare.

LIL: Don't tell. It's only the one. (*With another despairing look towards the door, in terror that* EUGENE *might come in*) Show me, Carlie.

CARLIE: I haven't time.

LIL: It won't take half a sec. You're so clever.

CARLIE: I lose my time, I lose my money.

LIL: I'll stay on after, do yours for you.

CARLIE: Why are you always, always round my neck?

LIL: Like a bad penny, aren't I? Like that coin up on the wall.

CARLIE: (*Weakening; she'll help*) I can't afford you, Lil.

LIL: Your kindness is only exceeded by your personal beauty.

CARLIE: I'll fucking swing for you.

LIL: (*Heart hammering, whispered, conscious that at any moment* EUGENE *might come roaring back and find them, willing* CARLIE *to be quick, to save her*) Don't worry, Carlie. You put me on the right lines, I'll see to everything. I will. (CARLIE *sits in* LIL's *place.* LIL, *one eye on the door, one on* CARLIE, *hovers anxiously. The machine roars smoothly.*)

The laceworkers' cottage. November 1840. MERCY *enters, holding the veil in its wrapping.*

MERCY: Four shillings he've took off our money.

FANNY: What?

ALICE: Eh?

MERCY: Four bloody shillings.

FANNY: Oh Lord, why?

MERCY: He've found a cinder mark.

FANNY: I never saw that.

MERCY: It's there all right.

FANNY: How did we miss it?

MERCY: I never should have let Fan try it on. I knew it. I never should have let us.

ALICE: A little dab of powder on that, or some chalk –

MERCY: He's not stupid.

(*They stand there, overwhelmed by this disaster, trying to visualize how it could have happened.* MERCY *looks suddenly at* ALICE.)

Were it you, Alice?

ALICE: Why me again? It was the three of us. We was all fooling.

FANNY: You was that end.

MERCY: Must have dragged it in the bloody firepot, and the cinders blow about.

FANNY: Last time it were warming her feet –

MERCY: That were more than a year ago.

ALICE: (*Realizing the truth, sinking*) I feel sick. There don't seem to be no blood in me.

MERCY: For two pins I'd larrup you till it ran down your back. Then you'd know.

ALICE: I'll put it right.

(*She crosses to the veil, picks it up and starts to search for the mark.*)

MERCY: That you will. And mind, Alice.

FANNY: Alice can't see nothing nearly.

ALICE: I can.

FANNY: You couldn't see the clock.

ALICE: I could.

FANNY: Jacob ask you and you –

ALICE: I could tell which was hands and which was figures. I've found it.

(*She peers at it, then goes back to her stool and starts to make a patch to cover the flaw.*)

I've got years of seeing left in me.

MERCY: (*To* FANNY) You'll have to take it to him.

FANNY: Not me.

MERCY: You. He ask for you special.

FANNY: Can't. I'm meeting Jacob. Up the quarry. There's a tree hangs down, and when the grass is tall –

MERCY: You'll go. He might let us off the four shillings.

FANNY: Bloody Alice. Dragged us under once again.

(*They work a while in silence. It is quiet but intense. They are all aware of what Fogerty has in mind for* FANNY. FANNY *is angry and frightened. When she speaks of Starlight she sees herself.*)

Starlight went to horse this morning. He bit her. Took a chunk out of her neck.

ALICE: Poor thing.

FANNY: She screamed so loud she scared the crows. They won't get a collar on her now, not for a week. Jacob tell me. He say the horse had a good time though. He say he went at it all right.

ALICE: Like you and him.

FANNY: Won't get my chance tonight. Thanks to you. Bloody Alice. Lord, I'm frozen.

MERCY: Wood's for cooking, not for warming.

(*They work on in silence.*)

FANNY: I'm that hungry, Merce.

MERCY: Still?

ALICE: (*Tentative – a peace offering*) I got an onion. Poor man's beef, my husband used to call it.

FANNY: Let's have some, then.

MERCY: Not till she put that right, you don't.

The sweatshop. Before lunch. As EUGENE *enters with* ANWHELA, CARLIE *slaps down the corrected pile of outworkers' jackets in front of him.*

CARLIE: Finished, Eugene.

(*She goes out to collect more work.* LIL *is hand-sewing.*)

EUGENE: Sew a bit here, sew a bit there. Can you do that?

ANWHELA: Oh yes.

EUGENE: Yeah. Here we're paid according to the amount we do – all muck in together. There'll be some statutory definition in some Section of some Act, there always is, but what it boils down to is, I give you a job, I give you a price.

ANWHELA: What work I did, it was very perfect.

(EUGENE *picks up a skirt from a pile on* LIL'S *table.*)

EUGENE: How many of these could you do in an hour?

ANWHELA: (*Examining it*) Eight.

EUGENE: Fifty-six quid.

ANWHELA: What?

EUGENE: On a good week when the sun shines.

ANWHELA: I am not a learner.

EUGENE: In the hand.

ANWHELA: You should get seventy, they said, at least –

EUGENE: Ah, but this is in the hand. No questions asked. Follow me? We'd be looking at roughly fifty-six. On a better week it's more.

ANWHELA: Fifty-six.

EUGENE: It fluctuates. Mostly it fluctuates down.

ANWHELA: My work is very first-rate.

EUGENE: The beauty of it is no stamp, no tax, no one gets their sticky fingers on it. Yours to play with. You can say yes or no.

ANWHELA: Well –

EUGENE: In the last analysis it's up to you.

ANWHELA: Yes.

EUGENE: Terrific. Lil, Anwhela.

LIL: Hallo, love. You'll be all right with me. Know all there is to know, don't I.

EUGENE: That's right.

LIL: Got stitching all along the line. Right back. My mother. And my mother's mother.

EUGENE: (*Echoing* LIL; *he's heard it before*) '. . . my mother's mother.'
(*He hands* ANWHELA *a balding broom.*)
Just give it a quickie. It's Em's job really, but –
(ANWHELA *sweeps round wherever she can.*)

LIL: Oh, Eugene, it'll be OK, won't it, to use the phone later? I'm sure he'll be OK, don't you think, he's such a tough old bugger, but –

EUGENE: Lil. Focus your mind. There's been a couple of times lately – not like you at all. One goes down, we all go down.
(*He's friendly, but he means it, and* LIL *knows and feels a prickle of fear.*)
There's another large consignment coming in. You girls'll have to handle it.
(*The phone rings.*)
Blockman's. Lace collars. (*As he hares off*) God. The shirt's running up my back like a roller-blind.

LIL: Listen, love, see if you can make sense of that chaos over there.

(LIL *points to a far corner where* ANWHELA *will have her back to her.* ANWHELA *goes over and starts to sweep there. Immediately, heart thudding,* LIL *goes quickly to Carlie's place. She again substitutes some of her own work for Carlie's. She covers a dreadful guilt with all the brightness she can muster.*)
This is your place. Used to be Naseem's. What's your name, love? Didn't catch it.

ANWHELA: Anwhela.

LIL: Pretty. Isn't that pretty? I shall call you Annie. This is my chair, Annie. This is my machine. And here's my cushion. I bring my own from home, the chairs are diabolical. We've been together a long time, my machine and me. It's like a marriage. 'We've been together now for forty years and it don't seem a day too much' – Except it's fifty-eight. You're doing that lovely. Em just gives it a smear of Dettol and a wipe-round. Her feet are gone, though.
(ANWHELA *stumbles.*)
Watch where your heels go. There's holes in this floor the size of dinner plates. (*Hearing* CARLIE *coming back*) Every time it rains we go for a paddle.
(CARLIE *enters with a huge pile of skirts.* EUGENE *follows with another.*)
Don't we, Carlie? Go for a paddle every time it rains.

EUGENE: All yours, darlings . . . (*Picking up the pile on Carlie's table which* LIL *has just added to*) These finished?

CARLIE: Yup.

EUGENE: Perfect, are they?

LIL: Of course.
(EUGENE *exits with the workload.* LIL *sees it go with relief.*)

CARLIE: Shut that door, one of you. It's arctic.
(*She and* LIL *sort through the new work, chalk it, divide it into three.*)

LIL: The wind blows terrible in here. We catch it off the river. You won't see me take my coat off, not for anybody. Not until August. Mind you, you think it's cold now. You ought to have been here in the old days . . .

CARLIE: Ah, here we go.

LIL: (*Paying no attention*) We used to have a tuppenny bucket of

21

coal, fan the flames with the cutter's bowler. But the work that went out of here – you should have seen it, Annie. Broderie anglaise, piqué, seersucker, real velvet. Mitred corners, tucks and flounces, finishing touches all over the place. The toilet's through there, Annie. Bring your own bog paper. Lavatory paper. Bring your own.

ANWHELA: I should go now?

CARLIE: Up to you.

LIL: Grab the moment while you can.

CARLIE: Grab the seat while you can. Lil's taken out citizenship papers in there.

LIL: When there's a rush on it's a luxury you can't afford. I'll lend you some of my bog paper, seeing as it's your first day. You can give me your biscuit in the tea break – OK? Naseem never had her biscuit, we had an arrangement. Talking of it's brought on the urge. You do this for me, love. Give me time to pop there first. (*On her way out*) And watch out for Rene. She's a slug.

ANWHELA: A what?

CARLIE: Rene. Big white-haired woman in slippers. With a white moustache. Stands outside the toilet counting the minutes – the seconds. For two pins she'd stand on her table and look over the top. She's star machinist round here. Toppled Lil a couple of years ago. So watch her. How many of these can you do?

ANWHELA: Eight.

CARLIE: Great. Let's go.
    (*They machine, in unison. Equal skill.*)
    (*Shouting*) This stuff's shit. Cloth's like iron.
    (*They stop. Adjust.*)

ANWHELA: So there is no test?

CARLIE: Sorry?

ANWHELA: Medical test. In my last place in the factory . . . all us Asian ladies and black ladies . . . there was a thing we had to do.
    (*They machine.*)

CARLIE: (*Shouting*) Oh yeah?

ANWHELA: (*Shouting*) Before we were allowed to have the job.

(*They dump. Pick up the next skirt.*)

CARLIE: What was it then?

ANWHELA: We had to give a sample.

(*They machine.*)

CARLIE: (*Shouting*) What, you mean on the machine? Run up a seam or something? Like a trial?

(*They stop. Adjust.*)

ANWHELA: No. A sample. A little tube of glass. We were to . . . we had to take it to the toilet and . . . we were to fill it.

CARLIE: Piss in it?

ANWHELA: Yes.

CARLIE: Why?

ANWHELA: To see if we were pregnant.

CARLIE: Bloody hell.

(*They machine.*)

ANWHELA: (*Shouting*) They sent away. You had to wait.

CARLIE: (*Shouting*) So what if you were? What's it to them?

(*They stop. Dump. Pick up the next skirt.*)

ANWHELA: They thought you would not work so well. So fast.

CARLIE: Why didn't they just ask?

ANWHELA: They said we would not tell the truth. Wanting the work so bad.

(*They machine expertly.*)

CARLIE: (*Shouting*) I don't believe it. I don't *believe* it.

(*They stop. Adjust.*)

My last one, the doctor said it'll get stuck in your ribs if you keep sitting cramped like that. She come out all right, though. Lovely.

ANWHELA: I did not want to work when I was pregnant. To be with men and to be teased because my –

CARLIE: (*Hearing* EUGENE *coming*) Watch it.

(*They machine.*)

EUGENE: Where's Lil? Three guesses. Lil!

LIL: (*Off*) On my merry way, Eugene.

EUGENE: (*Shouting*) Well, for God's sake get on with it. (*To* CARLIE) See what I mean? I'll have to let her go. I mean I love her, Carlie, we all love old Lil. But she's never in that chair, is she? Gone for a crafty smoke or lost a sleeve.

23

Machine's like a bloody tortoise. Her eyes are bad, her poor old heart's worn out, her indoor plumbing's on the blink. What do you think, Carlie?

CARLIE: Pay me boss's wages, I'll think like a boss.

EUGENE: How can I? Perhaps I should. I can't, can I? These old war-horses. Bloody ridiculous. Should be grazing in a meadow.

(EUGENE *exits. They machine, shout.*)

ANWHELA: That is not good for Lil.

CARLIE: If he fires her he'll kill her.

ANWHELA: Would you feel that way, Carlie?

CARLIE: Take a hell of a lot to kill me, love. Wouldn't half knock me about, though.

(EUGENE *steams in. They stop.*)

EUGENE: Where's that bloody address book? Every bloody thing in this place walks. I've just had Indira's husband on to me. Something's gone wrong with her operation. She's had her stomach stitched up backwards or some bloody thing. They've got to start on her again. God knows when I'll see her. So that's some more organization gone potty. I'm wringing wet, Carlie, I'm crucified. I don't know. You women and your innards. You'll be the death of me.

(EUGENE *races out again.* CARLIE *stamps down on her pedal again.* ANWHELA *follows. They yell to one another.*)

CARLIE: Bastard. How many we done?

ANWHELA: Four.

CARLIE: Great. I hope Lil can keep up.

(LIL *enters silently, watches as the two machines race.*)

I just hope she can do it.

(LIL *watches in fear.*)

The laceworkers' cottage. August 1841. FANNY *is four months pregnant. It's dinner time. They've finished their bread and scrape. Outside the door summer blooms.*

MERCY: I'm still starved.

FANNY: Alice, go and steal some apples. I dare you.

ALICE: All right. I will.

(ALICE *darts out.*)

MERCY: Alice! Oh, hell. There's Fogerty. Out there.

FANNY: Where?

MERCY: Up on the ridge. Best come in, Fanny.

FANNY: He won't see me.

MERCY: He will. And he'll catch Alice.

FANNY: He's miles away.

MERCY: He've warned us.

FANNY: Bugger him. Wish you could have seen my Jakey when he said goodbye. He had his flannel shirt on, the blue one like his eyes, sleeves rolled up – I could have ate him.

MERCY: I could eat anything. Oh come on, come on inside, Fanny, damn you. If Fogerty catch you with the door open we'll all pay.

(MERCY *is shaken with her cough, bends low.* FANNY, *seeing, immediately comes in.*)

FANNY: You in the dumps, Merce?

MERCY: I seen that doctor yesterday. Told him now it's in my chest, the pain, my sides, I can't breathe like I did. No wonder, he say, your organs is cramped up, your lungs don't have free play, that's why you cough.

FANNY: Oh, you can cough all right.

(*They laugh.*)

MERCY: (*Laughing*) Do you go to church, he say? Go to church, Mercy, pray.

FANNY: (*Crossing to her, hugging her*) Poor old Merce.

MERCY: (*Laughing*) Plenty of food, he say, plenty of God's fresh air and cut down on your work.

FANNY: (*A burst of laughter.*) That's ripe.

MERCY: No fool like a clever man.

(*Suddenly* MERCY *stops laughing. In a harsh whisper* –)
Christ! He's coming this way.

FANNY: (*Rushing to the door*) Alice!

(*She freezes.*)

MERCY: Come inside!

FANNY: (*Frozen, whispering*) I can't.

MERCY: Now. Come now.

(*They whisper.*)

FANNY: If I move he'll see me. I don't dare turn. Where is he now?

25

MERCY: Under the oak.

FANNY: Oh hell. What's he doing?

MERCY: Nothing. Staring at the hills. Like he'd all the time in the world.

FANNY: Bugger. Old bugger.

MERCY: Damn you, Fanny. If he take more money off us – damn you, I'll – (*Gasps.*) He's squatting!

FANNY: Eh?

MERCY: Doing his business.

(FANNY *gives a great explosion of frightened delighted laughter.* MERCY *shakes quietly.*)

FANNY: He'll get his bum stung with nettles. Bet he shit cow-pats.

(*They both giggle helplessly.*)

MERCY: He's up. He's off. Oh dear, I've hurt myself not laughing. Oh dear oh dear. Now you stay in, and don't you never do that to me again.

(FANNY *comes inside. She stops, puts her hands on her stomach.*)

FANNY: It moved. Oh, it's the sweetest feeling.

MERCY: Fanny, you're a fool.

FANNY: He said he'd write.

MERCY: Why haven't he, then?

FANNY: He will. He give me a bobbin box and carved me these. (*Showing* MERCY *a pair of bobbins on her pillow*) See? 'I Long To See My Love Once More' and 'Dearest Girl'. We walked along the river. His brown arm were round me –

MERCY: I'll bet he knew. Before he went.

FANNY: He said I were his one girl.

MERCY: You'll find out.

FANNY: He had to go. To London.

MERCY: That's worlds away.

FANNY: He say we must have money. You don't understand. Jacob have dreams. You've nothing in your life, he say. I have, I say. I got the bobbins and I got you. That's enough. He say that's bloody nothing. You think that's how things ought to be? It's not. He have these dreams. His back's got skin like a girl's.

MERCY: You had your joy and now you'll pay.

26

FANNY: I don't show, do I?

MERCY: No.

FANNY: Oh Mercy, all I want's to be with him and lie with him and have his arms round me.

MERCY: Give me a pain, you do.

FANNY: Oh. It moved again.

(ALICE *bursts in with three windfall apples. She has eaten most of hers already.*)

ALICE: (*Laughing, proud*) I thought he saw me take them. Feel my heart, it's banging like a drum.

FANNY: Oh, don't they set your teeth on edge. Still. Good, though, eh? Wish it was St Catherine's Eve tonight.

ALICE: Oh yeh.

FANNY: Beef in place of caterpillars.

ALICE: Mutton.

MERCY: Pork. Baked and boiled puddings.

FANNY: Warm beer spiced with rum.

ALICE: Egg beat up in it. Frothing.

FANNY: Oh don't.

MERCY: (*To* ALICE) Here, don't throw that (*the apple core*). I'll have it. I get that hungry.

ALICE: It's the consumption.

MERCY: I know it.

FANNY: I'm always hungry.

ALICE: Oh, you. You've a hole in your belly.

MERCY: Bet she wish she had.

(*They laugh and eat.*)

The sweatshop. Lunchbreak. A bell rings. All work stops instantly.
LIL *goes to unwrap her lunch at the ironing board.* CARLIE *is reading a bright, large, first year in secondary school book on Ancient Greece.* ANWHELA *starts to unwrap her food at her table.*

LIL: Here. You can't eat there.

ANWHELA: Why not?

LIL: You might muck up the cloth. You stand here, lovie, if you want to eat. Better here. You can rest your back, standing.

(EUGENE *enters with the pile of jackets. He dumps them on* CARLIE's *place.*)

EUGENE: These are all wrong, Carlie.

CARLIE: (*Examining them*) They're not mine.

EUGENE: They've got your tickets on.

CARLIE: These are not mine. I know my own stuff, Eugene.

EUGENE: The fairies come in the night, did they, mucked all the tickets up?

CARLIE: I'd never botch a job like that. They're diabolical. Try Vi, or Em, or Ernestine. (*Slams them down.*) Get on to the upstairs lot.

EUGENE: It's the third time, Carlie.

CARLIE: I bloody know it's the third time, and someone's cheated me three times.

EUGENE: Let's just say, then, until we find the culprit, let's just say they need unpicking and they need putting right and would you very kindly be the one to do it. Pronto.

CARLIE: No.

EUGENE: Carlie. I'm asking nicely. Please.

CARLIE: Why the hell should I?

EUGENE: (*Putting them back in front of her*) They've got to be put right.

CARLIE: You do them. You fucking do them.

EUGENE: We don't need emotion, Carlie.

CARLIE: Yes we fucking do.

EUGENE: I can hear the blood booming in my ears. That's a bad sign.

CARLIE: These are not mine. They weren't mine last time. Nor the time before.

EUGENE: Carlie. Shut up. Just do it. Hear me? Just do it. Or else.

CARLIE: Fucking fucking fucking fucking fucking fucking hell.
(EUGENE, *driven by* CARLIE's *rage, runs off. A silence.*)

LIL: (*Quiet*) Poor old Carlie.

CARLIE: Oh fuck. I'll have to bloody do them, won't I? Got so many bloody kids –

ANWHELA: You have many children, Carlie?

CARLIE: Six. Four at home, two off my hands, in squats. (*Laughs.*) It's my own fault. Breathe between my toes, I'm anyone's.

LIL: They've nearly all got different fathers. I love hearing.

CARLIE: That's all over now. I'm a reformed character. And just before we leave the subject, Lil, I know it's my tickets, what I said, and what I keep on saying is they're not my work. All right? If it's anything to do with you.

LIL: He has got up your nose.

CARLIE: Him and you both.

(*A silence.*)

LIL: Where were we? Oh yeah, our love-lives. I was no angel, me. Eugene's father used to say the boys are round you, Lil, like bees round a honey-pot.

ANWHELA: Why did you never marry, Lil?

LIL: I had six brothers, dear.

ANWHELA: Ah.

LIL: Then of course they went. One by one. Len was the last. The baby.

CARLIE: You should have went and all.

LIL: Shut up. Then there was Mother. But Maurice skims the worst off —

(*The lights go out.*)

Bugger.

ANWHELA: What is it?

LIL: The blooming lights have fused.

CARLIE: Not again.

(CARLIE *and* LIL *find their torches — this is a ritual they are used to.* CARLIE *shines hers for a moment on the workpile, stares at it furiously, then makes a conscious effort to forget it, at least during lunch. Though she tries hard, she is pulled back to it throughout the scene, and* LIL *and* ANWHELA, *one guilty, the other a newcomer, try to distract her anger.*)

The axeman called Saturday. Our electric. Cut us off.

ANWHELA: I have paraffin.

CARLIE: Lyle's bronchial. I can't have paraffin. Every bloody year the winter catches him.

ANWHELA: Here all the year is winter.

LIL: Maurice has to have the heating. That cat's no good without a radiator.

CARLIE: I said to the kids last Saturday, we're not sitting here in the dark listening to the rain plop on my stove, I says, so I bundle the lot of us into bed, head to toe, the kids are singing, we're eating sausages, I'm telling stories, and bugger me, the bed collapses. So there's another bastard. Anyway, Willa's dad come round, did a little operation on the meter.

ANWHELA: How did he do this? I should like to know.

CARLIE: Dunno, Anwhela. He broke a wire, I know that. Then he took the top off, fiddled about, put it all back where it was, and bingo, we could see each other.

LIL: Well, you've got to choose, haven't you? Be miserable or be criminal.

CARLIE: (*Shining her torch at* LIL) Which did you choose? (*She kicks moodily at a table.*)

ANWHELA: Our room is always dark, everywhere is dark. When I landed it was February and it was foggy and everything and raining, raining, and I thought oh my God where am I? I felt sad like anything. I cried a lot. My husband said now you are raining too so we laughed together. We held each other and we laughed so much I thought the baby would be born. The neighbours beat upon the walls but still we laughed and laughed.

CARLIE: Willa's dad'll show your old man.

ANWHELA: He's . . . he's away now. Business matters.

CARLIE: He's always been good with his hands. Willa's dad. Willa's the same. Good with the fiddly bits.

LIL: She'd be OK at this lark, then.

CARLIE: (*The torch beamed straight at* LIL) Good with the fiddly bits, are you, Lil?

ANWHELA: It is good to have a daughter to carry on if you are ill.

CARLIE: Trapped in a bloody dump like this? Over my dead body. She's going to be a barrister, keep us all out of trouble. (*She is back by her workpile, seething.* EUGENE *scurries in with his torch, hurls down some boxes from the shelves, starts to search through desperately.*)

EUGENE: Panic stations, girls. Lace collars. They've got to be round here somewhere. (*He dumps some boxes down in front of the* WOMEN.)

30

I finally tracked Stan down, they're not in the van. God in Heaven, why me? Why aren't I part of the Divine Plan? I swear God's fingering me.

(LIL *and* ANWHELA *open a box each and peer in.*)

Lace collars. Carlie, thought you'd have your nose to the grindstone.

CARLIE: (*Not moving*) After my break.

EUGENE: Lace collars, lace collars. Blockman's are going barmy. Come on, Carlie.

CARLIE: (*Not moving*) That stuff was not mine.

EUGENE: Hatchets buried, Carlie. All for one and one for all. If ever there was an emergency – I don't know. If I'd cut even slightly off-grain, I said, you'd be down on me like a ton of bricks. True?

(CARLIE *mooches over and joins in half-heartedly.*)

We got charts, I said, we got quality control, you're not talking to some bloody villain –

CARLIE: Who'd lop an inch off the bottom.

EUGENE: Right. Well. Anyway.

(*The phone rings. He calls out –*)

Mrs Khan! Tell Rene to take it up there. And I'm out.

(*Slumps into the nearest chair.*) Oh God.

ANWHELA: Are these the ones?

EUGENE: Anwhela, you're beautiful. You've given me back a year of my life. God bless you, dear. (*Springs up, rejuvenated.*) Right, girls. (*Taking the collars*) Onward and upward. (*Turns at the door, suddenly still.*) I'm watching you, Carlie. I tell you, it's The Day of the Jackal.

(*And he's gone.*)

CARLIE: Watching me. Bastard. What do I have to do to make him believe me? That stuff is not mine, Lil.

LIL: It's a mystery all right.

CARLIE: Don't need the Sweeney on it. It's one of the wrinklies, isn't it? One of them crafty idle crones has swiped my work and swapped the tickets round. I'll swipe her when I find her. And I will, I will find her.

(*A silence.*)

LIL: I dreamed last night I had it off. With the Duke of

Edinburgh. We had tuna fish sandwiches. Then he helped me turn out my kitchen cupboard.

ANWHELA: It is very good to dream of fish.

LIL: It's not bad having a bang with royalty.

ANWHELA: There is much luck in dreams.

CARLIE: Is there? Swing some my way, will you? Look at it (*the wrong work*). For the love of Christ will you look at it. Look at it.

LIL: I'll give you a hand, Carl. The end of the day, OK? I'll help you. Hey, them lace collars reminds me – told you I'd bring it in, didn't I?
(LIL *takes out from her pocket some tissue paper. Unwraps it lovingly. Inside is a lace traycloth.*)
There. That's a heirloom, been in the family since Queen Victoria's wedding. My gran made this.
(*The* WOMEN *touch it. Feel it. The* LACEWORKERS *stir. Their lights come up.*)
Real lace, this is.

CARLIE: If we had some windows we could see the sun on it. If we had some sun.

ANWHELA: How? It's dark.

CARLIE: Outside it's noon.

ANWHELA: You forget, don't you?

LIL: They say you can read lace like a book if you know how. My gran had it rough all right. Worked all the hours God sent, she said. If they fell asleep they got their faces rubbed in pinheads.

The laceworkers' cottage.

FANNY: Your face'd scald for days.

The sweatshop.

LIL: Told you we was stitchers, didn't I? A whole long line of us.

ANWHELA: It's beautiful like anything. You are lucky, Lil, in such an ancestry.

LIL: Yeah, it's bred in you, that sort of skill.

ANWHELA: And you, too, still at your table.

32

LIL: We're all goers, dear.
CARLIE: Didn't they do things lovely then?
LIL: That *periwinkle*, see?

The laceworkers' cottage.
ALICE: I done well to move here, out the factory.
FANNY: That's mine, I say. That's my leaf. I done that. No
bloody machine. You don't understand. Real lace'll move.
Machine-made is flat.
ALICE: No, it's not. It's even.

The sweatshop.
CARLIE: Makes this muck look silly. Still. We got a trick or
two. I can finish off a facing blindfold.
LIL: She can.

The laceworkers' cottage.
MERCY: It'll come, though. It'll come. Never mind you can't
even tell who made it. They'll find a way to say look what I
done. Look how it hang or how it last. They'll have to. You
put your whole soul and strength into a thing, you have to
find a pride in it, to stop yourself from screaming.
FANNY: If my child's a girl she'll work the lace. And her girl
too, and hers.

The sweatshop.
LIL: The shadows of our lives is in it. That's what gran used to
say. This was a bedspread once I think. I know its had bits
lopped off it as the years have gone. Don't we all? A
bedspread, then a tablecloth, then a table runner. Now it's
my traycloth. Suppose it'll end up a bloody hanky.
(*They laugh.*)

The laceworkers' cottage.
MERCY: You'll see. It'll come.

The sweatshop.
CARLIE: Right. Let's get this lot out of the way.

LIL: Thought you weren't going to work in your lunch hour.

CARLIE: Shut up. Then I'll start on Eugene's rubbish.

(*Sitting at her table,* CARLIE *is lit up, excited. She has a skill of her own.*)

ANWHELA: Should you not wait for the light?

CARLIE: You're joking.

LIL: Carlie could run you up a wedding dress under water.

(CARLIE *roars through a couple of garments. The lights come on. They whoop and cheer.* EUGENE *speeds in.*)

EUGENE: Right, girls, how are we doing? (*Seeing* CARLIE *still has a huge amount to get through*) God in Heaven, Carlie, you've hardly begun.

(*The phone rings, off.*)

Coming. I'm coming.

(EUGENE *leaves. A silence.* CARLIE *rises, stalks away from her machine, seething.*)

CARLIE: Those were not mine.

LIL: (*Very quietly*) Here we go.

(LIL *takes back some more of the work that needs unpicking, puts it on her own table.*)

CARLIE: We've got to be paid minimum time rate for God's sake. If we was in a union – it only needs three of us.

LIL: Oh God.

CARLIE: We need some clout. Bang the tins together. So someone'll hear us.

LIL: You won't change a thing.

CARLIE: I can bloody well try.

LIL: I don't want a raise. I'm all right as I am.

ANWHELA: He took me without a card.

LIL: I get my tax reduced, my rent reduced, help with my electric, if I got more I'd lose.

ANWHELA: I must repay him for his kindness.

CARLIE: Kindness! He took you, like Lil, because you're cheap.

ANWHELA: No, Carlie, no. I need to be here. I am grateful. One time I was a homeworker. It was terrible. I got so fat. And sick. Cook, sew. Eat, sew. Watch television. So many ladies. In so many rooms. Like battery hens. Never again. Never. I want to stay. I shall stay here as I am.

LIL: Right on, Annie. If you don't like it you can always leave.
CARLIE: I fucking hate that attitude. It stinks. All you old
wrecks – you're a waste of taxpayers' money.
LIL: Go put your head in a bucket.
CARLIE: No fight left in you. You can't even do it. Can you?
LIL: I can't do it? Me? You're barking. So obsessed with your
bloody union –
CARLIE: Fact. You can't do it. And if he finds out you've had it.
LIL: Don't you worry about me, mate. And don't you lose us
what we got. Annie and me, we're fine.
CARLIE: After all the dirt and all the din, I'm three pounds
better off than someone on the dole.
LIL: Three pounds is better than nothing.
CARLIE: Is it? Eating where you work. Stinking sinks. Stinking
toilets.
LIL: Sit on a piece of paper. You're in clover. We used to have
the rats jump right up and eat the ham roll out of your
hand. You don't know you're born.
CARLIE: You shouldn't be here at all.
LIL: I've more right than you. I was sitting here, girl, long
before you was thought of.
CARLIE: Right. You've had your turn. So go to the library, have
a warm. Go for a creep round the park. Go and play bingo.
LIL: I don't play bingo.
CARLIE: Well, learn. You ought to be plonked down, the lot of
you, in front of your favourite television programmes and
SHUT UP.
(*A silence.*)
LIL: I'm you later on, Carlie. That's all. (*Pause.*) See, if I was to
come in one morning and there was a girl at my machine –
it'd be like a ghost. Like I'd died.

The laceworkers' cottage. The WOMEN *chant in unison, very quietly,
under Lil's next speech.*
FANNY, ALICE and MERCY: (*Together*)
    Twenty pins have I to do
    Let ways be never so dirty
    Never a penny in my purse

35

But farthings five and thirty
(*Then nineteen pins . . . eighteen . . .*)

The sweatshop.

LIL: I'm walking down the end of the lane, Carlie. I don't know
what's down the bottom but it's bloody dark, I tell you. A
bloody dark cold wind. With a bit of luck it'll be a long
time before you have to look down there. But I haven't got
that long. So don't you come in here with your young arm
and try to sweep me off the table. I don't want the library. I
don't want to creep around the park. And I don't want – I
got to get on that phone.

(LIL *runs off.*)

The laceworkers' cottage. September 1841. ALICE *rises, blunders
desperately towards the door.*

ALICE: Mercy. I can't see.

MERCY: What?

ALICE: I can't see. There's yellow streaks before my eyes. Bits.
Jigging and dancing.

(MERCY *and* FANNY *have caught* ALICE, *held her.*)

MERCY: Oh, Alice.

FANNY: How many buttons have I?

ALICE: I don't know.

FANNY: (*Urgent*) Come on. How many?

ALICE: (*Peering*) Eight, is it?

FANNY: Four. How many fingers?

(*She holds up two.*)

ALICE: Four.

FANNY: How many now?

(*She holds up three.*)

ALICE: Six, is it? No, can't be six. Five. No, six. Oh, I don't know.

FANNY: She's seeing twice over. That's why her leaves was wrong.

MERCY: You been on the lace too long, Alice.

ALICE: I know it. What'll I do?

MERCY: Nothing you can do, except leave off it.

ALICE: How can I?

MERCY: You'll be at a standstill soon.

36

ALICE: Sometimes they burn terrible. Whatever shall I do?

MERCY: Don't know.

FANNY: Get a man.

ALICE: Who'd go to bed with a hump?

FANNY: You could sing in the streets.

MERCY: Whatever it is, best do it soon.

ALICE: It's clearing now.

MERCY: It'll come and go for a while. Do something soon. You get left behind, Alice, you'll pull us all down with you.

The sweatshop. Early afternoon. CARLIE *and* ANWHELA *are machining. They stop as* EUGENE *enters.*

EUGENE: All right. Where is she, then?

(*Neither woman answers.*)

Three guesses. Toilet, toilet and toilet. Well, put her on the pressing when she comes. Rene's timing the new style in the break.

CARLIE: Get Rene off it, then.

EUGENE: It's her job.

CARLIE: She's too fast.

EUGENE: Carlie, darling, don't make a battle out of it. Do me a huge favour.

CARLIE: Then have someone else but Rene do it. Save yourself some aggro.

EUGENE: I'm in no shape for battle. I know you're longing to crack all my bones. (*Crossing to the door*) My glands are up like grapefruits.

(*He leaves.*)

CARLIE: That'll slaughter Lil. Rene timing the new style. She's rattled enough already.

ANWHELA: It worries me. I can't afford to fall behind.

CARLIE: Least there's your old man working.

(ANWHELA *says nothing.*)

No?

(ANWHELA *says nothing.*)

No business matters?

ANWHELA: I have not liked to say. He could not earn enough for us to live on. So he was ill. He had a nervous breakdown.

CARLIE: No bloody use to you, that.

ANWHELA: He was so loving and so jolly. Now he cries. For weeks and weeks he cries.

CARLIE: Lucky we're stronger than men.

ANWHELA: A nervous breakdown is very terrible.

CARLIE: We haven't time for nerves.

ANWHELA: The man he worked for said you are here to work, not to be ill. If you want to be ill, go back home.

(LIL *enters slowly, sits at her place.*)

CARLIE: Oh. You're back, then. Eugene says get stuck into the pressing.

LIL: Do the pressing. Right. (*Goes slowly to the ironing board.*) It's like a fridge in here.

CARLIE: Eugene's idea. Work harder, keep you warmer.

LIL: I'm working so hard it's a strain on my heart. Lucky it's a big one.

(*She tries to laugh.*)

CARLIE: Rene's timing the new style in the break.

ANWHELA: Not long now.

LIL: Oh God. (*Stops pressing.*) Have you seen it? Is it a bastard? Is it ruffles? Is it?

CARLIE: It's tricky.

(LIL *starts pressing again.*)

ANWHELA: You look ill like anything.

LIL: It's that damn cat. His kidney's gone. He's supposed to have all white meat. How the hell am I going to do that – I mean chicken and fish, they cost a fortune.

ANWHELA: Creatures are very strong, Lil.

LIL: Yeah, he's a tough old bugger.

ANWHELA: A little egg in milk is very good –

LIL: Yeah. You're right, Annie.

(*She picks up a fresh garment to iron, presses it.*)

CARLIE: Lil. For God's sake. The other bloody side.

LIL: Don't shout, you'll make me worse. Oh, I see. The other way. Got it. D'you know, I had a ribbon in my school hat the exact same red as this. I saw a lovely boy in church once. And he saw me. He did. I left my hat behind so I could go back, get another look at him. Held his head like a

king, that boy. Used to go to dances, hops, you know. Any
dance you'd find me there in the centre, hair flying, legs
twinkling away.

(*The tea break bell goes.*)

CARLIE: Anwhela, get Lil a cup of tea.

(*The moment* ANWHELA *has gone* LIL *moves urgently towards*
CARLIE.)

LIL: Carlie. Do me a favour. Show me how to set these.

CARLIE: Sorry, Lil. I got this fucking lot to do (*her pile of
rejected work*).

LIL: Please.

CARLIE: Lil, I just said –

LIL: All the bits keep wandering.

CARLIE: Like your mind.

LIL: I keep thinking about that damn cat. See his face. Please.

CARLIE: (*Rising*) I ought to get a medal.

LIL: I know. I'm terrible.

(CARLIE *sits at Lil's machine. Runs it a moment. Demonstrates.*)

CARLIE: It's the top shoulder. Not the centre. Your nips should
be together. OK?

LIL: OK.

(*She changes places with* CARLIE. *Runs the machine. It's
wrong.*)

It's awkward. Getting your mind round the changes. (*Tries
again.*) The top . . . not the centre . . . (*It's wrong.*) One
more time?

CARLIE: I've shown you forty times.

LIL: Let's make it forty-one.

(CARLIE *changes places.*)

God'll reward you. If He's looking.

(CARLIE *machines.*)

CARLIE: Not the centre shoulder.

LIL: Not the centre shoulder.

(*She tries. Fails.* CARLIE *goes back to her place.*)

CARLIE: What's the point?

LIL: My mind slips. It's like a landslide.

CARLIE: Telling me.

LIL: You shouldn't be so hard.

39

CARLIE: I can't take you on, Lil. I can't risk my job for you. I'm middle-aged, I'm skint, I'm on the skids. Don't give me your grief, I got my kids to feed.

(*As* CARLIE *sits with a sigh at her place and pulls her pile of rejected work towards her, Rene begins offstage to time the new style. Her machine goes in smooth bursts. The* WOMEN *listen tensely, everything forgotten.* ANWHELA *comes in with Lil's tea.*)

LIL: She's started.

ANWHELA: The new blouse?

CARLIE: (*To* LIL) Check your watch.

(*They listen.*)

LIL: What's it like? You seen it, Annie?

CARLIE: The collar's tricky. Frilling. Twin needling.

LIL: Oh God.

ANWHELA: Is it always Rene?

CARLIE: She's the star turn.

LIL: She's a bloody wizard.

(*They listen.*)

Listen to her go. Please God make her hands cold.

(*They listen.*)

CARLIE: 'She's round the armhole and she's round again – now she's coming up the straight – '

LIL: It isn't fucking funny.

CARLIE: No.

(LIL *and* ANWHELA *listen.* CARLIE *goes back to her work.*)

LIL: Fiddly, is it?

ANWHELA: Double frills set into the cuff.

LIL: Rolling the edge'll be a bastard.

(*They listen.*)

Let it all pile up on her. Let her threads break.

ANWHELA: Don't worry, Lil.

(*Rene's machine roars smoothly on.*)

CARLIE: Here. Hang on.

LIL: What?

CARLIE: I don't believe it. This stuff Eugene brought in – it's the same thing – the shoulder – rucked up the same way – this was your fuck-up. You swapped the tickets, didn't you – all this is your stuff.

(*She goes for* LIL.)

LIL: I never meant to land you in it – Carlie – on my life I –

CARLIE: (*Lashing at her*) Three times.

LIL: You're hurting me.

CARLIE: Hurting you? I ought to kill you.

(ANWHELA, *trying to help, to part them, gets lashed as well.*)

LIL: (*Escaping*) I got behind, you see.

CARLIE: Laying it on me, you bastard, losing me time, getting
Eugene on to me –

LIL: I'm sorry, Carlie. Never again. Swear.

CARLIE: Why don't you stop trying? Just get out.

LIL: What'd I do? All I got is what I do.

CARLIE: What's that, eh? What do you do? Apart from fuck me
up. What, eh? Listen to the kettle boil?

LIL: You'll be old one day.

CARLIE: You're clutter.

LIL: You might be old for years. They're getting so clever at it
now.

CARLIE: Time you was swept away. You should be smashed up
on the rocks before you drown the rest of us.

LIL: You'd like that, wouldn't you? All tidied under our little
green mounds with our little white crosses –

CARLIE: Yeah. I bloody would. I've two kids on the dole, never
had a job, give their eye teeth for the chance –

ANWHELA: She's stopped (*Rene's machine*).

LIL: You've upset me.

CARLIE: Good.

LIL: My heart's banging –

CARLIE: Don't start playing Eugene's record.

LIL: Anyway, he'd never let me go.

CARLIE: Who says?

LIL: He says.

CARLIE: No, you. You're the one that says it. Think back.
Always you.

LIL: That's not true. You're jealous, that's your trouble.
Jealous. Because I was his father's right-hand man. Because
I'm irreplaceable.

CARLIE: You're cheap.

41

LIL: You wouldn't know. You're just another pair of hands to him. He loves me.

CARLIE: Fifty quid a week for a forty-hour week. No wonder he loves you.

ANWHELA: Carlie, Lil, oh please.

LIL: I'm his best girl.

CARLIE: You're a woman. For Christ's sake, we're women. You haven't been a girl in a long time, Lil. A long, long time.
(*A silence.*)

ANWHELA: Please. She's stopped.
(EUGENE *enters.*)

EUGENE: Lil. Could you come here – have a word?
(*He looks at her, at the other* WOMEN, *turns and leaves.* LIL, *head high, follows him.*)

ACT TWO

The laceworkers' cottage. MERCY *is showing* FANNY *and* ALICE *a parchment draught – a pattern.*

MERCY: We'll cover this with *blossom filling*.

FANNY: I like *blossom filling*.

MERCY: And *ladder trails* here. Whole-stitch edge and half-stitch flowers.

FANNY: What here?

MERCY: Trolly net. *Scallops* here. And *diamond filling*.

FANNY: Lovely.

ALICE: You done it good, Mercy.

MERCY: We got *acorns* here, see, half-stitch, and *acorns* whole. And *bullocks' hearts*. And *turkey tails*.

FANNY: And *periwinkles*. I'll do them.

MERCY: Reckon it should take us about two thousand hours. That's what I tell Fogerty. Fourteen hours a day – three of us – so long as Alice don't pull us back –

ALICE: I won't. I won't.

FANNY: Ellie Pluck say splash a drop of whisky on your eyes. That sharpens them a while. Or dog piss.

MERCY: Don't look to us to cover for you.

ALICE: No. I won't.

MERCY: You're not quick enough, that's your fault. You'll have to be left behind.

The sweatshop. LIL *bursts in, followed by* EUGENE.

EUGENE: I had to do it, Lil. I had to.

CARLIE: What's up?

LIL: He's took my skill away from me.

EUGENE: I had to cut her rate. Her and Vi.

LIL: He has. He's broke my pride.

ANWHELA: Poor Lil.

EUGENE: The pay's related to the skill, it has to be – if you can't keep up –

ANWHELA: How could you do it to her?

EUGENE: Why am I the villain? Anyone'd think I was fucking Rumpelstiltskin. Six of these on time. That's all. If she

can do it she's entitled to the minimum piece rate. If she
can't –
CARLIE: Piece work should be bloody abolished.
EUGENE: Don't look at me. I didn't make the system.
CARLIE: It's diabolical.
ANWHELA: The fear of it, always pushing like a beast behind
you.
EUGENE: You can do it. Carlie. Em. All the old girls except Lil
and Vi. Even Ernestine. They can all trot out six.
(*Stricken, he turns to see* LIL, *collapsed in grief, rocking silently
backwards and forwards, and crosses to her, kneels to try to
comfort her.*)
Come on, Lil. You've got to face it. Anyone can stitch. Any
old mother can sew.
(*A silence.* CARLIE *and* ANWHELA *stare at* EUGENE
stone-faced.)
(*Gently*) Lil, they make the money up top. That's how it
works. They can stick on anything they like. Three
hundred per cent. Their profit margins are astronomical. I
have no jurisdiction over that.
(LIL *hasn't moved at all.* EUGENE *hugs her.*)
Lil, my stairs are crumbling, I owe the finance company,
my wife cries every night.
(LIL *hasn't heard.*)
CARLIE: We've got to stop this –
EUGENE: You can never stop it. Never. We're animals, that's
all. Belligerent animals. We may suddenly have a
conscience. On occasion. Been going on, though, hasn't it,
since Adam and Eve. Look, Lil, all I know is I've got to
keep my production line going and if I don't make a profit
we can all forget it.
ANWHELA: We'll take a cut.
EUGENE: Know what a real competitive wage'd be? Carlie? A
Third World wage. I can't do that. There's parts of this city
that's Third World enough already. I won't add to it.
CARLIE: If we was in a union –
EUGENE: We can't afford to strike. You've got to be strong to
strike. There's no strength in this lark. That's why it's

44

bound to be low paid. No skill. No strength. Not talking about cars, are we, or building sites, or oil. That's where the bargaining power is, in the heavy stuff. Power goes where the money is, money goes where the power is. God in Heaven, clothes are flimsy. Clothes are women's stuff. Women's stuff'll always get lost at the back, won't it? A woman's not the breadwinner, is she? Pin money.

(*A silence.*)

ANWHELA: What's going to happen to her?

EUGENE: Anwhela, every single morning I think this is the day we're going to collapse. All these old ducks looking at me, relying on me. I tell you, I wake up drenched. We've a chance, nothing more, but a chance, if every single one can turn out six on time.

(*Suddenly* LIL *raises her head. She is still, sure, strong.*)

LIL: I can do it.

EUGENE: Lil –

LIL: I can do it.

EUGENE: Don't let's go through this again –

LIL: I can.

EUGENE: Come on, girl.

LIL: Time me. Go on.

EUGENE: I don't want to hurt you, Lil.

CARLIE: Go on.

ANWHELA: Give her a chance.

CARLIE: Go on.

LIL: Time me.

(*Slight pause.*)

EUGENE: Give her the stuff, someone.

(ANWHELA *collects a pile of skirts. She lays them in place on Lil's table.* LIL *is to sew zigzag trimmings on to the skirts.* LIL *rises, crosses purposefully to her table.*)

LIL: (*To herself as she crosses*) Dear oh dear.

(*She sits at her machine, rubs her hands, flexes her fingers.*)

Saw one of them underwater programmes once. *The Sea About Us* – something like that. They had these coral branches. Made out of millions of tiny fish – beautiful. Just like my hands.

EUGENE: Time's money, Lil.

LIL: (*Strong still*) Just talking my nerves down, Eugene, won't be a tick. Don't look so good when it's your hands, better when it's coral.

EUGENE: Right then.

LIL: Right then. Here I come. Living dangerously.

EUGENE: (*Eyes on his watch*) Let's go.

LIL: (*Straight at* EUGENE, *baleful, challenging*) Wish me luck.
(*She switches on her machine. Rests her hands on it for a moment as a concert pianist might before playing.*)
Right.
(*She machines. They watch. She goes fast. Smoothly, expertly, she whips each garment through, a star performance from a star. One either side of her table,* CARLIE *and* ANWHELA *count as she speeds through each one – one, two, three . . .*)

CARLIE: You're pushing it a bit.

LIL: All right, all right, I know what I'm doing.
(*On the fourth skirt now, and* LIL *is really fast. The material piles up, the needle jams, snaps.*)
Oh God, oh look at that. Oh God, what a bastard.
(*Frantically changes the needle.*) You need a new machine, you do. Bloody old thing.
(EUGENE *says nothing, eyes intent on his watch.*)
Buggering thing.
(LIL *machines again. It goes steadily and well. She finishes the fourth. She relaxes. It's getting faster. She steams through the fifth.*)
(*Bellowed, raging, triumphant, straight at* EUGENE) Who says I'm sub-ordinary now? Eh? Who says I'm past it? Eugene?
(*She's on the sixth. It's very fast.*)
'Call me early Mother dear, for I'm to be Queen of the May – '

CARLIE: Watch it.

ANWHELA: ⎫ You are going too fast.
EUGENE: ⎭ Calm down for God's sake.
(*The material piles up.*)

EUGENE: Get your foot off the pedal. OFF THE PEDAL!
(*The machine has jammed again. Silence.*)

46

LIL: It's just today. Maurice is on my mind.

EUGENE: It's not today, Lil. Sorry.

LIL: I haven't done this one before. Things come up before I'm ready for them.

EUGENE: You can't do six.

ANWHELA: Five she can do.

EUGENE: Not six.

LIL: I'll get better. Soon as I get used to –

EUGENE: If you only sew five you're –

LIL: Sub-normal.

EUGENE: Sub-ordinary. Speed, Lily girl, that's all. Nothing personal.

LIL: You keep changing things. I don't know where I am.

EUGENE: That's fashion, Lil. Shake the kaleidoscope. The world keeps wanting change.

ANWHELA: It takes time to learn a pattern.

LIL: I'll get the hang of it.

EUGENE: By then it'll be time to learn another.

LIL: How'll I go on?

EUGENE: God, Lil –

LIL: I don't know how I'm going to go on.

EUGENE: We're all just lurching from one calamity to another. If you knew –

LIL: You've took away my pride. You shouldn't do that.

EUGENE: You're still my dear old Lil. Aren't you? And this place would be nothing without you, we all know that, so let's get back into production for God's sake. Come on, girl.

LIL: (*Starting to cry*) You shouldn't take away a person's pride. It's like you're asking me to stop living.
(*She goes to blow her nose on some material.*)

CARLIE: (*Automatically, before she can stop herself*) Don't *do* that.
(LIL *takes out a handkerchief. An avalanche of buttons fly out with it and roll across the floor in the long silence.*)

EUGENE: Jesus Christ.
(*They stare at each other.*)

LIL: Oh. Where did all them come from?

EUGENE: The fairies, Lil? Under the gooseberry bush?

LIL: Well, that's a mystery.

47

EUGENE: If you want buttons come to me and ask.

(LIL *says nothing*.)

Don't make yourself look cheap. It's me. Eugene. I know all the strokes.

(LIL *says nothing*.)

You can have as many as you like. What have you got there – couple of hundred? Have them all – all we got. Anwhela, get the boxes.

(ANWHELA *doesn't move*.)

Ten thousand? Twenty thousand?

(EUGENE *rushes to the button boxes, slams some down in front of* LIL.)

Start a button boutique – an emporium – that what you want? Is it? Start a fucking button empire.

(*He kicks some of the buttons on the floor towards her*.)

LIL: I'd have put them back.

EUGENE: Can you hear yourself? Can you?

ANWHELA: I think you should leave her.

EUGENE: How do you think I feel? Lil. Of all people. After all these years. I want to cry and that's the truth. Christ, it makes me sad. Why, Lil?

CARLIE: Pack it in, Eugene.

EUGENE: I've always said, you want a remnant, come to me and ask. Don't walk out with it wrapped round you like something from *The Curse of the Mummy's Tomb*. Trust. We run here on trust. Buttons. It's so stupid.

LIL: Right. I'm putting them back. Look.

(*She stoops, picks up as many as she can. The others watch in silence*.)

Can't have rolled far. (*Finds some more*.) I'm finding them all over.

EUGENE: Lil, they're yours. My compliments.

LIL: Where's the box?

(ANWHELA *hands her the box and she tips a handful in. Then stands alone while the others collect some more*.)

EUGENE: For God's sake keep them. They'll have the filth of all the world on them from off this floor.

LIL: Like me. I'm the filth of all the world to you.

48

EUGENE: What the hell's come over you?

LIL: Me and Vi – you're not satisfied to see us crumble day by day, that's not enough, you have to wound us, take away our pride.

EUGENE: For God's sake, Lil, sub-ordinary's just a word. It means –

CARLIE: She knows what it means. It means 37p a blouse instead of 50.

LIL: It means the water's closing over my head. It means I'm rubbish, all my life's been rubbish. Stuck here like a rat in a cage –

EUGENE: 'Look after Lil,' my dad said and by God I have –

LIL: Scuttling backwards and forwards, picking up a crumb now and then –

EUGENE: No one else would, I can tell you. Out of kindness.

LIL: Don't make me laugh. For the first time it's crashed in on me – I'm cheap. Carlie's right. I'm cheap and old. I'm clutter.

ANWHELA: Why do I not take her home?

LIL: By God I'm cheap. You owe me a lousy sodding button.

EUGENE: Lil, can this be you?

LIL: You fucking owe me.

EUGENE: I'm glad my father isn't here to see –

LIL: He never would have treated me like you. He was a gentleman.

EUGENE: That was another world. It wasn't dog eat dog then, people were buying, people paid a decent price –

LIL: All my life stuck in this rat hole –

EUGENE: If you felt like that why didn't you go?

LIL: I stuck it because you've got to stick it. When you're us that's what you do. Stick it. Sit here quiet with our necks bent while the world passes over our heads. Well, now I've had enough. (*Sweeps all she can off her table.*) Where's my life gone? Oh, dear Christ, where's it gone?

In the laceworkers' cottage the lights find FANNY, *then* MERCY *and* ALICE. LIL *freezes.*

FANNY: If I had the ordering of the world, if I was God, we'd be

princesses. Live in a castle. We'd have gold rings, and a
bird in a cage, and fruit in a big glass bowl.

MERCY: There's rain on the hill. I love that hill. Reckon I'll be
under that hill soon. All the dead round here lie in that hill.
When I go, I want to be put away all nice. Snug in a box.
And put my lustre jug in with me, and my clock.

CARLIE: Tell you my dream. My own place. Mine. Somewhere
to dry my things. A bit of grass at the front for the kids to
play. I'd take the kids and me on holiday, somewhere nice
and hot. See the pyramids and where the Greeks and
Romans were, see history. I'd meet a man who'd like the
kids and fucked the socks off me. Then I'd come home,
turn the key in my own front door. Put the heating on
when I want some heat, and off when I've had enough.

ALICE: Know that stream? I'd like to jump right in that stream
and walk down it till it's a river and then on down that river
till the edge of the sea, and lie down in the sea and sleep in
the waves.

ANWHELA: I would like all day to be Sunday. Sundays are so
nice. I have friends round, we play cards, we play guessing
games, we have some cakes and little sweet biscuits, we
laugh.

FANNY: I'd have myself a toasted herring. Every day.

ANWHELA: I want to go home. Our house was small, it had no
door, but we had a little land. We ate three chickens in a week.

MERCY: An apron full of corn for the geese.
FANNY: And a belly full of bacon pie.
ALICE: Oh, you and your bacon.
(*The lights on the* VICTORIANS *fade.*)

LIL: I want what I had. I want my long hair and my friends and
dancing. I want to be wanted. I don't want to be in slow

motion no more. Creeping like a beetle up a chair leg. I want to belong somewhere. It's not enough to kiss the baby's head. I want it like an ache, more than anything on God's green earth.

ANWHELA: Someone do something –

LIL: (*To* CARLIE) Where's the fucking rainbow, eh? (*To* ANWHELA) Where's the pot of gold?

CARLIE: Anwhela – tea, quick.

(ANWHELA *hurries off.*)

LIL: There's nothing, is there? All my life is nothing. Only buttons.

CARLIE: Come on, love. Never mind the bloody buttons. Come and sit down.

LIL: And they belong to him.

EUGENE: Lil, pet, let's all sit down and –

LIL: I'll give you all I've got. The lot. The lot.

(LIL *picks up a large pair of scissors. During the next speech she slowly, deliberately hacks the buttons off her coat. She is quiet, but there is murder in the air.*)

It's good. It's quality. Double-stitching. Hand-finished round the collar and lining. Tiny stitches – shouldn't be seen in a rat hole like this. I have it on my bed. Maurice used to keep me warm nights, but he's gone now. Damn cat. Damn thing.

(*She has folded the coat neatly. She slams it down in front of* EUGENE.)

Been a friend to me, this coat. A good coat's an investment.

EUGENE: Lil – for the love of God –

(LIL *has returned to the scissors and methodically attacks her skirt buttons. Gradually it drops to the floor and she stands with it around her feet.*)

LIL: (*Cutting the buttons*) This come from my nephew's girlfriend's school jumble sale. Never liked it. Always had someone else's shape in it. I don't like the feel of someone else's shape been there before you.

(*She steps out of the skirt, folds it, adds it to the pile in front of* EUGENE.)

EUGENE: Lil, can't we find a way to –

LIL: (*Sawing at her cardigan buttons*) Bought this one summer, maybe fifteen, sixteen years ago. Me and my brother Len that lives in Coulsden, we went on a coach outing to the country. Oh, we had a day. We sang, we paddled in a stream, we saw a dragonfly. That was a day all right. (*She folds her cardigan and adds it.*)

CARLIE: You'll catch your death. There's a hell of a cold wind – (LIL *is concentrating on taking off her sweater.* ANWHELA *comes in with a cup of tea.*)
Eugene –

EUGENE: I don't know what to do. (CARLIE *takes the mug of tea from* ANWHELA *and offers it to* LIL.)

CARLIE: Have some of this. Warm your cockles. (LIL *ignores them. She is struggling with her sweater over her head.*)

ANWHELA:⎫ Please, Lil.
EUGENE: ⎭Do you good.

LIL: (*Folding her sweater with care*) This was mother's. When we was kids we was so cold. Poor old mum. Poor old her. Creeping about looking for warmth, for blankets, for some kindling.
(*She adds her sweater.*)

EUGENE: Talk to her, someone. (*The silence stretches.* LIL *is undoing her blouse.*)
Listen, Lil. Remember when we made that dress and when we put it on the dress stand it was huge? Rene made a mistake in the pattern – remember, Lil?

CARLIE: And you said, bollocks on it, why not make it double-breasted, and we did, and we got away with it. They took it.

EUGENE: And we all leapt about because we never thought they would. Queen for a day all right that time, Lily Marlene. Sherry all round, twenty fivers in the hand, and that was then. Remember?
(LIL *has hacked off her blouse buttons, folded the blouse.*)

LIL: (*Placing the blouse on top of the pile*) Cheap fabric. Seconds. Isn't even on the grain.

EUGENE: (*In a small, appalled whisper*) That stuff's ours.

(LIL *stands there in her vest and bra and slip*.)

LIL: Remnant. Left in a corner, thrown out in the end. Like me.

EUGENE: For God's sake, Lil. No one's thrown you out.

(ANWHELA *crosses to* LIL, *takes the scissors from her, puts her own coat round* LIL's *shoulders and leads her away*.)

LIL: I got a prize at my school for my smocking, did I tell you, Annie?

ANWHELA: I should like to have seen it. Very much.

LIL: Wish I was young now. Wish I was still at school. Fifty-eight years I been here.

(*She stops, turns back in, moves down to* EUGENE.)

See me. Acknowledge me.

EUGENE: Lily, I do.

LIL: I'm not who I was. Course I'm not. But at my own speed I still got the skill.

EUGENE: Lil, in another time, another place –

LIL: But nobody wants it, do they? Not any more. You could have saved me. You could have said, no one can touch your smocking, Lil, your buttonholes is perfect. But now we got machines can do it just as good – well, maybe not as good but it'll look all right, we'll get away with it. So seeing as you're so special at it, what we'll do, we'll teach you something else you can be good at, something these things can't do. We'll educate you. Train you. But no one ever said that, did they? Not your father, and not you.

EUGENE: You're supposed to pick it up as you go along.

LIL: That's not sewing, is it? That's feeding a machine. No time to think. No time to make a proper job of it. Just sit there with your heart banging in your ears and them things screeching. Stop knowing who you are and what you are and who you used to be. Who was I, Eugene? Was I really someone?

EUGENE: You were an artist.

LIL: Now I'm sub-ordinary. Now I'm getting 37p.

EUGENE: I'm truly sorry, love.

LIL: What am I supposed to do? Live on a box of cottons and my memories?

EUGENE: It's not my fault. It isn't like it was.

53

LIL: What have I done wrong? Except get a bit older. Will one of you please tell me? What have I done wrong?
(*A silence.*)
EUGENE: Lil, you're a hiccup on my production line.
LIL: I work my guts out for you – and all I am's a hiccup? You bastard, Eugene, you rotten, stinking bastard. You've left me on the sand. You've took my skill away and left me on the sand and I got nothing. A stupid old carcass to lug about all day. And nothing. A smile, a slap on the rump, a cup of tea – a fucking cup of tea. Nothing.
EUGENE: The world's moved on, Lil. You don't understand. Sat there stuck in your old dream –
LIL: It's you that doesn't understand. Not one of you. Look. These hands is just a cover. My real hands is inside them. And they're stitching away, quick, quick, quick. Fifty-eight years I've sat there. All my working years. I've stitched my life away for you. You've broken my whole life.
(ANWHELA *moves tentatively towards her.*)
Leave me alone. Leave me alone. For God's sake. All of you.
(*The others look at one another uncertainly.*)
Please. You got to. Please.
EUGENE: Go on, girls.
(*He ushers them out. They hurriedly collect their things together, one eye on* LIL, *who seems calmer now, just lost in thought.* LIL, *alone, stands still. The lights dim.*)

The laceworkers' cottage. December. A baby cries. The WOMEN *make their lace.*
MERCY: It's waked.
FANNY: It's hungry, isn't it? The poor thing's empty.
ALICE: Go dance it about a bit.
FANNY: It make it sick.
(*The baby cries.*)
ALICE: If I close my eyes I can see a web. A golden web. It's beautiful.
MERCY: You mind your work, Alice. Never mind closing your eyes. You keep them open while they're still some good to us.

54

(*The baby cries.*)
Don't look off, Fanny.

FANNY: I won't. I won't.
(*The baby cries.*)

ALICE: Don't fret, Fan.

MERCY: When it cry you turn your head, see. Lose stitches. We mustn't lose our stitches.
(*The baby yells.*)

ALICE: Hear it bellow.

MERCY: She's not the time to nurse it proper.
(*Unable to bear it,* FANNY *slams her pillow down on her stool and goes up to the corner where the baby is.*)

FANNY: I feel it in my belly when it bawl.

MERCY: (*Suddenly, the words torn from her*) Lizzie Pomfret gave her baby Godfrey's Cordial.
(*A silence.*)

FANNY: Lizzie Pomfret's baby went and died.

ALICE: That were the fever took it off.

FANNY: So she say.

MERCY: A spoonful of that and they don't cry no more. Lay there like little dolls.

ALICE: You can get on. Go to the chemist, I should. He'll give you a bottle, wrap it up in paper for you. Penny a week.

FANNY: How'll I find that?

ALICE: You pay into the funeral subscription, don't you? Well, don't, then. Put that penny by.

FANNY: It died. Its face went flat and yellow and it died.

MERCY: We're trying to help you, stupid. You dug your pit, we're trying to find a way up out.

FANNY: It's Jacob's child. It's pretty. It wave its little fists about –

MERCY: Stop that. You want too much. You don't want to kill it. All right. But you can't keep it like it is, you got to quiet it. You can't have a child and keep up with your work. You can't. That's asking for the moon.

ALICE: Feed it the Godfrey's, stick it in a corner and get on.
(*A silence.*)

FANNY: It's not right in the sight of God.

MERCY: Only the rich say that.

ALICE: Give it a bit of a push into the next world. There it'll be right close to God's sight. Anyway, it might not die. They don't all slip off.

FANNY: I don't want Jacob's baby half idiotic. Like Maria. Like Annie May. A booby gaping in a corner.
(FANNY *shivers*.)

In the sweatshop LIL *also shivers*.

FANNY: It seemed such a bright thing, loving him.
(*She sways, sobs*.)

In the sweatshop LIL *mirrors her movements, sways, gives a muffled sob*.

MERCY: No use to cry.

FANNY: Last night I saw a jacket on a nail. Thought it were his.

MERCY: He's not coming back.

FANNY: Lord, I don't want to go downhill.

MERCY: (*Putting her shawl round* FANNY, *helping her on to her stool*) You better rest. Not for long, mind. You should have taken up with Fogerty.

FANNY: Never.

ALICE: In the end, if your eyes don't hold out there's nothing for you but your body. Have to be quick, though, before your breasts fall and your belly wrinkles. He gave Ellie Crick a sovereign and some linen.

FANNY: No doubt she earn it.

ALICE: She says he'll buy her a watch next. You'll be in clover.

FANNY: I hate him. He don't care who we are or what we are or what we feel or what we think or how we live. All he want is the work done and the work done and the work done and that's all.
(*She tries to rise, falters*, ALICE *and* MERCY *help her, sit her again*.)
I'm not as strong as I thought I were. After the birth of it.

MERCY: Row with the stream, Fan. It'll quiet it.

FANNY: It'll make it sick.

MERCY: We're all sick, girl, one way and another.
  (*A silence. The baby whimpers.*)
FANNY: What's in it, then?
ALICE: Only treacle boiled in water.
FANNY: There's opium in it. That's what sleeps them.
ALICE: Why do you ask, then, if you know?
FANNY: It rushed so quick into the world. Like it were keen to
  look about.
ALICE: Don't know what for. Nothing for it here.
  (*The light in the cottage fades.*)

The sweatshop in darkness. 8 p.m. LIL *sits motionless.* CARLIE *enters.*
CARLIE: Lil? That you?
LIL: Oh. You jumped me out of my skin.
CARLIE: What are you doing here?
LIL: Looking. You know. Thinking. Memories.
CARLIE: You all right? Thought you'd gone home hours ago.
  Eugene said you were OK – he'd had a word – we would
  have hung about, but –
LIL: Yeah. He had a word.
CARLIE: Good.
LIL: He understood. Said I could stay a bit. So long as I didn't
  waste the lights.
CARLIE: Bugger that.
  (*She switches them on.*)
LIL: He had something a bit desperate on. He's coming back to
  lock up when it's sorted.
CARLIE: Got all the way home and find I've left my shopping
  here. We're eating African tonight. Had to come trolling
  back – got almost to my door – hadn't you better get your
  things back on?
LIL: Oh yeah. Forgot.
CARLIE: Sure you're OK?
LIL: (*Still bright, still convincing*) I told you. I'm all right.
CARLIE: Left the lot. (*Collects two carrier bags.*) All the
  emotion . . .
LIL: That's all over now. I'll have to get poor Annie back her
  coat, she'll get frostbite.

CARLIE: Eugene let her go home in the van. Bring it in the morning.

LIL: In the morning. Yeah. He's done it, Carlie.

CARLIE: What?

LIL: He's done it. Eugene. He's give me my cards.
(CARLIE, *by the door, is stopped. Turns back in.*)

CARLIE: What?

LIL: He has.

CARLIE: Bloody hell.

LIL: For my own good, he said. I need a rest.

CARLIE: Well, bugger me.

LIL: He's given me my wages with a vengeance. And my holiday pay, have that, he said, that's yours. And my Saturday's. Been quite good really.

CARLIE: Terrific.

LIL: He has. He give me these twenty tenners straight. On top. In the hand. Twenty tenners, Carlie, there'll be a couple of people pleased about that.

CARLIE: The little shit.

LIL: Thought you'd be really chuffed.

CARLIE: Why?

LIL: Well. You know. Doddery old prune. All that.

CARLIE: Oh, me. I've got this stupid great big mouth. But all those years –

LIL: Maybe I'll take to it, giving up work. (*Starts to pack into her carrier bag her tape measure, scissors, her cushion.*) Think I will? Maybe I'll pack myself in, go down the road in style, go in a taxi. They're very good there, give you your own pot of jam with your own name on it. Mind you, I don't like to think of not having an address, not being at number sixty-three –
(*Her legs suddenly give way.* CARLIE *rushes to help her up, sits her down.*)

CARLIE: Oh God – Lil – here –

LIL: (*To herself*) Come on, Lil. No use to cry. (*To* CARLIE, *who has knelt beside her*) Funny. I used to want to live a long life. Like a tree. It says that in the Bible. In Isaiah. You shall do that, it says.

CARLIE: Oh yeah.

LIL: God, Carlie, it's like I've collapsed inside myself and I'll never get out again. Trouble is, I'm not worth anything. You shouldn't go on living if you're not worth anything, should you?

(*She grips* CARLIE'*s wrists desperately*.)

CARLIE: Who's worth anything? I don't know. What a question. God knows.

LIL: Does He?

CARLIE: Eh?

LIL: Does God know? What do you think? Is there a God or isn't there?

CARLIE: If there is He don't give a monkey's bollocks about you and me.

LIL: What I ask myself is, why did He put me on this earth if it's not to be useful?

CARLIE: In order to screw you.

LIL: I can't believe that, Carlie.

CARLIE: They've got to have a whole load of people they can screw and spit on or there'd be nobody to do the work.

LIL: You don't have to spit on me to make me work. I like it here.

CARLIE: 37p? Scum money.

LIL: Well, it's his job really, isn't it? Give us as little as possible. That's his job.

CARLIE: Jesus, you're wet.

LIL: I'm tired, Carlie.

CARLIE: You're being spat on.

LIL: Suppose I am really.

CARLIE: And it's never too late to see it.

LIL: Yeah. You're right.

CARLIE: Come on. You're not ready for pennies on the eyes yet, remember?

LIL: You're right. I should have told him what I thought of him.

CARLIE: That's more like it.

LIL: Wish I had. Wish I'd kicked him.

CARLIE: That's the spirit.

LIL: I should have given him a real good kick. I should have killed him. (*Struggling to her feet*) Just let me at him. EUGENE!

CARLIE: (*Catching her, trying to restrain her*) He'll have gone home an hour ago –

LIL: EUGENE! 'Sub-ordinary'! You lying bastard.

CARLIE: Lil –

LIL: Past it, am I? I'll show you.

CARLIE: Lil –

LIL: He owes me. (*Breaks free of* CARLIE's *grasp.*) He fucking owes me.

(LIL *heaves one of the bales of cloth out and flings it across the room.*)

Bastard! Right. Who's next? When you come to think of it there's loads of them. Carlie!

CARLIE: There bloody is and all.

LIL: Bastards who should have their heads stuck in a bucket.

CARLIE: You're on.

LIL: (*Flinging another bale*) My dad.

CARLIE: Your dad. (*Hurls a bale across.*) That bloody rent officer.

LIL: That bloody rent officer. (*Flings another bale.*) Them toads up the Council.

CARLIE: The toads.

(*The bales fly. Together they race to attack piles of garments, boxes, anything.*)

All the mean, thin-lipped, grasping bullies –

LIL: (*Throwing*) All the rusty, dusty tat –

CARLIE: (*Throwing*) That's for all the kids who've just left school and can't get nothing –

LIL: (*Throwing*) All the shabby rags –

CARLIE: All the people stuck in dumps like this –

LIL: (*Scattering a pile of bills and leaflets high in the air*) That's for me.

CARLIE: (*As they rain and flutter down*) All of us.

LIL: All of us.

(*Exhausted, triumphant, ablaze with shared excitement they stand gasping for breath, laughing with one another, among the chaos. A slow cross-fade.*)

The laceworkers' cottage. February. The LACEWORKERS *hold out their christening robe.*

MERCY: Well. There we are. And a day to spare before the christening.

ALICE: Won't he look grand, Squire's babe? So many stitches.

MERCY: So many sorts of stitches. *Honeysuckle* –

FANNY: See my *periwinkles*?

ALICE: *Peacocks' tails.*

MERCY: *Acorns. Roses.*

ALICE: *Crowns.*

FANNY: Most of them *periwinkles* is mine.

MERCY: This is the most beautiful thing the human hand can make and there's no boast.

ALICE: That's God's truth, that is.

(FANNY *folds it carefully. There is a small whimper from the baby.* FANNY, *holding the robe, crosses up to it.*)

It won't hold out long.

MERCY: Two days?

ALICE: A week.

MERCY: Look at the way it breathe. Be under the grass in two days. Let the snow make a winding sheet for it.

ALICE: The ground's hard for burying.

MERCY: Throw it in the quarry.

FANNY: No. Not the quarry. Jacob and me, we –

MERCY: Don't think. Let the water have it.

FANNY: The trout'll get to her.

ALICE: Only her body.

FANNY: Pick her clean.

ALICE: She'll be in Heaven.

FANNY: Course she won't. She's not baptized.

ALICE: The soul of a babe flies up.

FANNY: Do it?

ALICE: Nothing to stop it.

(*A silence.*)

FANNY: I'll give her to the water, then. Anyway, I don't like to see them stamp on the clay.

(*They stand looking at one another helplessly, nothing more to be said.*)

MERCY: Come on. Best mind our work.

(MERCY *and* ALICE *go back to their lace.* FANNY *stands, holding the robe like a child.*)

FANNY: Think of it looking up at me under the ice. Hope its ghost don't come back at night and walk about and frighten me.

MERCY: (*Taking the robe from her*) Don't cry. A tear on the work'll stain.

FANNY: Poor old babe. Wish I knew a prayer for it.

MERCY: Alice'll know one.

ALICE: Me? Why me?

MERCY: I seen you in the churchyard, muttering to the stones.

ALICE: I don't know no proper prayers. I just keep asking for a bit of life left in my eyes.

FANNY: I used to pray ever so pretty once. Can't remember what.

MERCY: Don't dwell on it, Fan. One more look, eh?

(*They unfold the robe again.* FANNY *holds it.*)

ALICE: You know me. Makes me want to cry.

FANNY: I don't want to cry. I want to shout out in front of all the world – I made them *periwinkles*.

ALICE: Fanny and her bloody *periwinkles*.

FANNY: They're mine. I done them. Like a man'll do a painting and be proud, well, I done this.

MERCY: Well. There we are. Two thousand hours, near enough.

ALICE: Fourteen hours a day.

MERCY: Last for ever.

(*The baby whimpers.* FANNY *turns up towards it.* MERCY *catches her hand, holds her back, gentle, firm.*)

ALICE: Squire's grandson'll be a little prince in it.

(*She and* MERCY *watch* FANNY *anxiously, needing to encourage her, needing her to return to work.*)

He will. You can be sure this one won't be sent out to work as soon as he can crawl.

(ALICE *and* MERCY *laugh.*)

MERCY: Fourpence a week, tuppence back for schooling.

(*They laugh.* FANNY *breaks away, goes up to stare down at her child.*)

FANNY: The lace care nothing for nobody.

MERCY: Why should it? We made it and it's beautiful and that's enough.

(*Suddenly resolute,* FANNY *turns back to face them.*)

FANNY: Is it? Well, not for me.

(*She hands* MERCY *back the robe, turns to face* LIL *in the sweatshop.*)

I'll have more than lace to remember me by.

(*Swift cross-fade.*)

The sweatshop. LIL *and* CARLIE, *panting, smiling, friends.*

LIL: We showed them, didn't we?

CARLIE: We did.

(*Suddenly the triumph leaves* LIL, *she is a small, defeated old lady. But only for a moment.*)

I would have helped you, Lil. It's just in here –

LIL: I know.

CARLIE: You don't have time –

LIL: I know.

CARLIE: It's made like that. To divide us.

LIL: Is it?

(LIL's *heart suddenly hammers painfully. A wave of dizziness. She leans on the table.*)

CARLIE: What is it?

LIL: It's all right. It'll go.

CARLIE: You ought to watch it.

LIL: (*Laughing*) What – stroll along the sands in the sunset? What'll I do? My stepping stones is all gone now.

CARLIE: Sorry?

LIL: Stepping stones. Morning, give the cat his biscuit. Night-time, fold his blanket down the end of my bed. So then you think, he's gone. Work. Get stuck into work. Now that's gone. What'll I do?

CARLIE: Learn something. Use your brain.

LIL: It's too late.

CARLIE: No, it's not. I'm learning off my kids.

LIL: I'm scared. Sat in the same place every day. My mind'll have the moth in it by now.

CARLIE: Give it a shake out. Put it in the sun.

LIL: Whatever you do goes ahead of you. I believe that. If we was making something beautiful, something that'd see us out, I wouldn't mind.

CARLIE: One day I'm going to have my own shop. Retail stuff downstairs, couture and made to measure up. Lingerie. Rose pink. Damask. Scarlet taffeta.

LIL: There's nothing I can leave behind me that can go ahead. When I'm gone, Carlie. When I'm not knocking about no more. All that effort. And there won't be nothing. I shall perish. (*Smiles across at* CARLIE, *picks up a bit of cloth.*) Like this. Limp. Scraggy. Look, no body to it. (*Rips it easily.*) Perished. We'll all perish.

(*It flutters to the floor.*)

There we are.

(*A slow dim.* ANWHELA *enters. She has a box of children's skirts. She sits downstage, and begins to sew a hem by hand, as fast as she can. There is a desperation about her sewing. The lights brighten.*)

In the VICTORIANS' *cottage the lights have come up too. They stand facing* ANWHELA, *motionless.*

In the sweatshop LIL *sits utterly still. She will not move again, and soon the group of women will hide her from view.* CARLIE *stands alone, upstage, facing away.* ANWHELA *runs out of cotton, has to scramble to find more.* FANNY *watches a moment, then crosses into the sweatshop to join her. She sits, smiles.* ANWHELA *passes her an identical child's skirt to hem.*

ANWHELA: Tiny little stitches.

FANNY: Yes.

(FANNY *sews expertly.*)

ANWHELA: Carlie!

(CARLIE *doesn't move or turn.*)

(*To* FANNY) Can you finish these sixty garments by tonight, he said. We need it like that. Carlie! Carlie, please.

(CARLIE *hears now, and moves down to join* ANWHELA.)

No matter how fast your fingers go, maybe two or three is left. Carlie –

(CARLIE *is with her now, and takes a garment and begins to sew.*)
My husband has gone, I don't know where. Perhaps he has
gone home.

FANNY: My Jacob went to sea. He had to.

ANWHELA: I should be home now, with my child, and look. All
these.

FANNY: I'd like to have gone to the sea for the day, picked
limpets off the rocks.

(ANWHELA *cries out. Her thread has come out of her needle.*
MERCY *and* ALICE *look toward her.*)
Merce!

(MERCY *leads* ALICE *across and they sit too. Now all the women
are sewing together, on the same garments. As they come –*)

ANWHELA: My hands were not made to be so quick, so quick.
It's terrible how quick.

ALICE: Twist and pin, twist and pin.

MERCY: Sometimes an inch a day.

FANNY: Give my soul for a glass of gin.

(*All the* WOMEN *sew fast and well, in unison.*)

ANWHELA: I shall save and save. Then I shall find my husband.

FANNY: I'm going to take my girl, make my way to London,
find my Jacob.

MERCY: Fogerty'd kill you.

ALICE: That man was sent by God to look after Fan. Took her
child in too. He'd give her anything.

MERCY: Except a ring.

ALICE: He lets her have two candles, even in summer.

MERCY: Watch your stitch.

FANNY: She can't.

ALICE: I can feel my way. It's easy.

ANWHELA: It must be nicely done. We must be ready. I told
this rent officer, my child must have a coat for winter, a
baby must be warm. That is your look out, he said.

CARLIE: Bastards. What are they anyway? Shadows. Tanya's
lost a shoe – OK? They can wait, her shoes can't. Tanya's
not a shadow. I can see her. She's mine. She's got thumbs
like mine. Her toes bend over the exact same way mine do,
she walks like me. She's mine.

(*They sew frantically.* FANNY *has finished hers, bends to get another from the box. She pulls out Lil's traycloth. She and* MERCY *stare at it, transfixed.*)

FANNY: Look! That's mine.

(*She hands it to* MERCY.)

I made that. That's mine. Them *periwinkles* – they're mine.

ALICE: Never!

(MERCY *hands it to* ALICE, *who feels it, smiles.*)

Beautiful.

FANNY: (*Taking it back, handing it to* ANWHELA, *who passes it to* CARLIE) I made that.

(*The* WOMEN *stop sewing in astonishment.*)

I did.

ANWHELA: But it's Lil's.

(*The lace* WOMEN *nod, smile at one another.* CARLIE *holds the traycloth, stares at it.*)

FANNY: If my child's a girl, she'll stitch. And her girl, and hers.

ANWHELA: Please. May we – ? (*Starting to sew*)

(*The* WOMEN *again begin to sew, needles flashing in and out in unison.* CARLIE *watches them.*)

CARLIE: What are we doing? What the hell are we all doing?

(*Slowly during Carlie's speech the* WOMEN *sew less and less, stop and listen.*)

This was Lil's. Poor old Lil. So proud. Stitchers right back along her line. And all she's left behind her is a bloody hanky. (*Holding out the lace to the* VICTORIANS) You put your whole life into a thing and this is all that's left – look at it – Christ! We've got to come out fighting. Swords in both hands. Oh, Lil, why aren't you here? We've got to shout.

MERCY: She can't now.

FANNY: She's too far away.

CARLIE: We've got to shout.